THE
WIDOW'S
BLOOD

THE WIDOW'S TRILOGY

THE WIDOW'S BLOOD

JENNIFER SCHULZ-JOHNSTON

JSJ
NORTHWEST PRESS

Books by Jennifer Schulz-Johnston

The Widow's Garden
The Widow's Secret
The Widow's Blood

I dedicate this book to B.M.R.
for daring me to love again.

ACKNOWLEDGMENTS

I would like to thank my sisters, Sarah and Rebecca, for being my faithful beta readers and my sounding boards for this endeavor; my late parents for encouraging me to believe in my dreams; and my nephews, Zach and Rowan, for keeping my imagination alive. I'm so blessed to be your blood. Thank you to my colleague, friend, and fellow author Mary Pierce for always supporting my notion that I could be a writer someday, and my Auntie Sue for the feedback, love, and smiles. None of us can accomplish very much alone. I'm so blessed by all of you.

What is life for? It is for you.

—Abraham Maslow

CHAPTER ONE

Claire

The wind whipped strands of hair across my face as I stared at the relic of a castle. Haunted. Auntie May had bought this haunted Scottish castle many years ago. The other students piled out of the van behind me, their chatter mingling with the howling wind.

A sharp elbow jabbed into my side. "Sorry," Julie muttered, not sounding sorry at all. I rubbed the spot, my gaze never leaving the foreboding stone structure.

Cold, damp air bit at my skin, the wind swirling relentlessly around us. We were eight art students sharing this space for the duration of our stay—ten weeks. The idea of sleeping in a room with four other women felt awkward, but as I stood before this daunting castle, the wind moaning around me, I felt relieved not to be alone.

"This is Scotland in June?" Rob's voice was tinged with disbelief. My classmates hurried ahead through the high yellow grass, eager to settle in, then find the nearest pub and get drunk.

"Are you coming with us, kid?" Barry called over his shoulder.

"No," I replied, feeling a wave of shyness.

"You're sixteen, right?" he guessed.

"Yeah," I said quietly.

"That's old enough over here, I think. You should join us, Claire."

"Thanks, but I'm tired from the flight," I explained, embarrassed by my timidity.

"No worries. Next time," he said with a shrug.

I heard Julie say something to Carissa, who laughed. Barry glanced back at me, rolling his eyes. I took his gesture as a sign of sympathy for me. My silk scarf whipped frenetically in the wind, threatening to fly away. I grabbed it just in time.

"Nice save," Barry said, waiting for me at the door.

The stone structure loomed with an icy, unwelcoming presence. The wind cut through me brutally, making the castle seem a haven in comparison. A shiver ran down my back as I took in the discolored stones, the castle now appearing far more likely to be haunted. Gray clouds hung low, casting a shadow that consumed everything in the vicinity.

Something whistled in the distance as the wind shifted. The piercing noise caused the hair on my neck to stand up. While the other students had disappeared inside, Barry and I kept a similar pace. He tucked his head against the cold as we moved in brief unison. I finally understood the allure of wool clothing. Also, my shoes were ill-suited for scampering through moors—my dad had always had something to say about my "interesting" footwear choices.

I picked up the pace, nearly turning my ankle on the uneven ground. Flailing momentarily, I regained my balance. Hopefully, no one saw that. I wasn't usually clumsy, but awkward? Occasionally. The shrill whistling grew louder, urging me to get inside. I closed the distance between Barry and me quickly.

He glanced up, a smile touched with impatience. I couldn't blame him. I rushed past him, murmuring thanks, catching a whiff of his cologne—a scent that made my stomach lurch.

Inside, Julie and Carissa cackled as they mounted the stone staircase behind a house staff member, who I guessed might be our housemother. I took in the massive fireplace, the elaborate candelabrum overhead, the horned skull mounts above the mantel, and the impressive Persian-style wool rug covering the stone floor.

The other students were already heading upstairs, captivated by our housemother's thick and melodramatic brogue. Her every word carried an urgent, panicked tone—even as she described the timed water heater. It was just her way of speaking, but it took a moment to acclimate.

Her words held us all spellbound as she detailed the dinner menu. I peeked into a modern bathroom with low ceilings and updated amenities, almost boringly so. Even the light fixture made me yawn in a state of underwhelm. My mother's taste for interior design had clearly influenced me more than I'd realized.

The housemother, Effie, led us to the room that we women would share. The ceiling was so high that I squinted to see the timbered rafters in the shadows, hoping nothing was nesting up there. Another enormous fireplace dominated the room, which held five beds. Each was made up with white sheets and pillows, topped with stacks of woolen blankets, many in tartan patterns. Feeling a deep chill, I hoped the sheets were flannel. I desperately longed for warmth and planned to add another layer of clothing at the first opportunity.

I was struck by the dampness that permeated the space. The cool, rainy days obviously dominated the weather pattern here, not adequately allowing this stony place to dry and air out completely. A subtle, musty smell infiltrated my senses at every turn.

Effie left our room after announcing when dinner would be served. My stomach growled at the mention of food.

With only us girls in the room, Julie commented, "It stinks in here. Can you smell it?"

Carissa nodded. Her nose wrinkled.

The other two students, Tiffany and Joy, quietly moved toward their respective beds with luggage in hand.

I busied myself, unpacking my clothes into the dresser nearest my bed.

Things were clean: the bedding, the dresser drawers, the floor. It was unfortunate about the smell, but I'd probably get used to it.

⁘

The dining hall buzzed with excitement as the cohort and I gathered around the long, heavy wooden table for our first dinner at the castle. Candles flickered along the stone walls, casting playful shadows, while the rich smell of roasted meat, buttery potatoes, and fresh herbs filled the air. Effie bustled around, her cheeks flushed and her eyes sparkling with mischief as she served each dish with a flourish.

My mouth watered at the smells and sight of what looked simply delicious.

"Aye, ye'll not find a better meal in all of Scotland," Effie declared proudly, setting down a steaming platter of lamb in front of Vic, who immediately helped himself to a generous portion.

Tiffany grinned, already halfway through her first serving. "Effie, I think I might cry. This is the best thing I've ever tasted."

Effie let out a hefty laugh, patting Tiffany on the shoulder. "That's the spirit, lass! But just wait 'til ye hear the tales this castle holds." She leaned in, her voice lowering to a conspiratorial whisper. "This place has more secrets than ye can imagine, I promise ye that."

Rob looked up, his curiosity obviously piqued. "Secrets? What kind of secrets?"

"Oh, well now, ye'll be wantin' the tales of the spirits that wander these halls, won't ye?" Effie replied, a gleeful twinkle in her eye. "Aye, there's spirits roaming all around here. They say the laird himself lingers in the west wing, searchin' for his lost love. And there's the maid who appears in mirrors, warnin' those who've lost their way. But it's Lady Red ye'll want to be wary of—she guards the castle's treasure, as folklore has it, and won't take kindly to anyone who dares disturb her peace."

Barry shifted in his seat, glancing nervously around the room. "Are you serious?"

Effie cackled, waving a hand at him before patting down an unruly silver hair near her haphazard bun. "Oh, there's nothin' to worry about, lad! So long as ye keep yer wits about ye and respect the spirits, ye'll be fine. Just don't go snoopin' in the hallways at night, or ye might find a ghost on yer heels."

Julie burst into laughter, nudging Barry. "Come on, Barry, don't tell me you're scared of a little ghost story!"

Barry huffed as if trying to appear unfazed. "I'm not scared! I just wasn't expecting to be haunted while studying art, that's all."

Effie grinned, apparently delighted by the reaction she'd stirred up. "Och, and that's just the tip of it, my dears! They say that spirits have taken a liking to artists—those with minds and hearts open enough to see what others canna. So, ye best be on yer guard."

Joy, wide-eyed but clearly enchanted, leaned forward. "Have you ever seen one of these ghosts, Effie?"

Effie gave her a knowing smile. "Och, I've seen plenty a' strange things here, lass. Spirits, shadows, lights that flicker in empty rooms. And more than once, I've felt someone walkin' beside me, only to turn and find no one there." She paused dramatically, glancing around at each one of us with a mischievous smile. "So, if ye hear footsteps at night or feel a chill down yer spine, don't ye worry. It's just the castle makin' sure ye're mindin' yer manners."

We all exchanged glances, torn between amusement and fascination. Vic leaned back in his chair, shaking his head. "Effie, you really know how to set the mood."

She winked. "Och, it's my job to keep ye all in line—and entertained!" With that, she rubbed her hands together vigorously. "Now, dig in! It's a long night ahead, and ye'll need all yer strength if ye're planning on crossin' paths with Lady Red."

Laughter and chatter filled the room once more as we returned to our meal, sneaking occasional glances at the flickering candlelight. I wondered what we might encounter in the ancient castle's shadowed halls. As I dug into Effie's culinary delight, the idea of sharing our new home with the spirits felt both thrilling and strangely comforting— thanks to the warmth of Effie's storytelling.

Effie brought another carafe of water to the table and added in a hush, "There's one more thing ye should know about these long summer nights here in Scotland." Her gaze swept over us, eyes sparkling with mystery. "Ye will notice that even in the dead of night, it doesn't get quite dark. The sky holds a kind of twilight glow, a shimmer that lingers just beyond the hills."

Carissa visibly shivered, glancing toward the tall, narrow windows that lined the dining hall. The sky outside was a deep, dusky blue, barely fading from the last glow of sunset.

Effie nodded, catching her glance. "Aye, it's beautiful, but it's also a time when the veil between this world and the next grows thin. They say the spirits walk freer than ever on these bright summer nights. And I'll give ye all fair warning," she continued, her voice low and rich with seriousness. "If ye see somethin' movin' beyond the windows, don't look. Don't stare. Don't let yer curiosity get the better of ye."

Barry raised an eyebrow, half-laughing but clearly intrigued. "Why not? What happens if we look?"

Effie's expression grew solemn, and she leaned in closer, her voice barely above a whisper. "It's said that the spirits can sense a gaze upon them. And if ye look long enough, they may look back and take a liking in ye. Once they do, it can be nearly impossible to break their hold."

A hush fell over the room, the clinking of forks and soft murmurs fading as we all glanced toward the windows. I wondered what might be lying just beyond the glass, hidden in that faint, eerie twilight.

Joy's eyes widened. "So, basically, don't make eye contact with any ghosts?"

Effie chuckled, though her eyes remained serious. "Exactly, lass. Just keep yer head down if ye hear something or think ye see movement outside. Sometimes, a spirit will fixate on someone who pays them too much mind, and ye might feel their presence lingerin' far longer than ye'd like."

Rob shifted in his seat, casting a quick, wary glance at the window. "Noted. No window gazing at night."

Effie gave a satisfied nod. "Good lad. And remember, spirits are like wild creatures—they've got their own ways, their own rules. Show respect, and ye'll do just fine here. But push yer luck . . ." She raised her eyebrows, letting the sentence hang in the air, her warning clear.

We looked at each other, a mix of excitement and nervousness flickering over everyone's faces. For a moment, I could almost believe that we were truly part of something otherworldly— some ancient, forgotten world held within the castle's walls.

"Well then," I said as a smile tugged at my lips. "We'll keep our heads down and stay on the good side of the spirits."

Effie winked. "Aye, ye'll have a summer ye won't forget."

Julie and Carissa chatted and cackled between themselves, choosing outfits to wear to the pub. I didn't see any wool ensembles being arranged. They were going to freeze.

I gave a start as Joy approached suddenly, asking, "Are you coming to the pub, Claire? I know you are in high school, but I don't think they care about that over here."

I smiled at her sweetness and answered, "No. I don't drink. Besides, I'm pretty tired, and I want to do some reading. I brought along a book that looks really good. I tried reading it on the plane, but I couldn't focus. I was too excited," I spilled in a hurried mash.

She returned my smile warmly, her eyes shining suddenly through the cloud of what I interpreted as sadness. She was pretty in a very innocent sort of way, and I couldn't help but pick up on a sense of vulnerability from her. Or maybe it was lostness, if that was a word. Yes, she had a lost quality about her.

"Oh," she said with a shrinking smile. I could feel her disappointment.

I felt bad. Fiddling with my diamond bracelet, the sweet sixteen gift from my parents, I offered, "I'm sure we can hang out tomorrow."

She recovered some of her smile and agreed with a nod, explaining, "I'm going to change my clothes."

"I hope you have fun. Be safe," I said and then immediately felt like my mom.

Speaking of my mom, she had been so eager to hear from me. I was glad I called her as soon as the plane touched down. She appreciated knowing that I'd arrived safely.

Julie, Carissa, and Tiffany gabbed loudly while donning their pub attire and fussing over their hair and makeup. This village was so small that I wasn't sure who they were trying to impress. Oh, wait. I guess our male compadres, Barry, Rob, and Vic, were viable suitors. Oh, funny. Or was it more funny that I wasn't attracted to any of them?

"Claire, why aren't you getting ready?" Julie arched an eyebrow and put a hand on her hip.

I cleared my throat. "I'm not going."

"Why not?"

I held up the book I planned on reading. "Hot date."

Joy chuckled while Julie sneered, and the others watched quietly.

A rap on the door grabbed our collective attention.

"You ladies ready?" one of the guys inquired through the majestic wooden door. It didn't sound like Barry. This voice had a hollow quality about it. Actually, the nasal engagement of this timbre matched that of Vic's voice, which I'd heard a couple times on the flight.

Vic was a quiet, observant fellow, it seemed. All three of them seemed nice enough. I couldn't wait to see the artistic ability of my cohort in the coming weeks and months. I had a feeling Joy possessed some real talent. She just put out that kind of vibe.

I remembered just then how my dad used to say that it was the way a person lived inside themselves that made them creative or not. I can't say I know exactly what that means, but on some level, it always made sense to me. I think it has to do with how you trust yourself. But anyway, Joy struck me as someone who trusted her innermost self. It was her eyes that said she had trouble trusting others.

"Almost!" Julie squawked a response to Vic's query and broke my train of thought.

"We'll be downstairs. See you in five?" Vic asked.

"Yes!" Julie said.

"Cool," he replied.

The four ladies looked decidedly pretty as they headed toward the door, flinging their purses over their shoulders as they scurried. Joy looked over her shoulder at me and smiled, waving quickly.

I waved at her and watched until they disappeared behind the closed door.

Quickly, I changed into my flannel pajamas, feeling chilled as cool air prickled my skin. I donned the fluffy bathrobe that my mother insisted I pack and snuggled into the woolen bedcovers with my book.

Before I could settle into the pages, my mind wandered. I thought about my twin sister. We usually liked the same things, moved similarly, and drew like-minded conclusions—each with our own unique twist. And let's be fair. I don't know what it's like to *not* be a twin. I imagine life can be lonely, flying solo, and I hope I never know for sure. This was the first time being so far away from Gini. I wasn't sure how to feel about it.

My sister and I had grown up with the most loving, attentive parents two kids could ask for. And our parents were in love every second of our lives. It was mushy, maybe even cheesy at times too. And I realized as I got older that my parents set the bar high regarding love—what it looked like and how it felt. I wanted to experience that kind of love someday. My short-lived high school sweetheart had never given me that feeling.

Anyway, here I was, having an adventure by myself. Sixteen years old. No parents. No boyfriend. No twin sister. In Scotland for the summer semester to study art in a castle with college art students. The only high school student: me.

Gifted. I'd been deemed gifted. At least artistically. A characteristic I likely inherited from my dad. And, perhaps, Auntie May, who knew her way around a canvas and paints as well.

Although, my mom was no one to sneeze at, being a best-selling author in her own right. OK, so I have two gifted, talented, successful parents as well as direct links to talented artists via my genetics. And as long as I'm comparing, my Auntie Livy and Uncle Nigel are highly successful and have gorgeous, brainiac triplet daughters. Then there's Grandma Ivy, whom no one can hold a candle to on any level. And last but far from least, my twin sister who is *summa cum laude* in everything. Yay.

Then there's me. Besides my art, I may as well be the family dog.

But art is cool, and maybe it will end up being enough. I can always hope. I keep hearing how artists don't make money until they're dead.

Well, my dad must be the exception because his dabbles and dawdles really went to the next level. His paintings of snooty, uptight, silly, ridiculous, high-society frogs took a New York art show by storm not long after my parents met. Or at least that's the story I've heard a thousand times. My parents enjoy the re-telling of their love story. They drive me crazy sometimes, but that's their job, and it's my job to make them worry, apparently.

Me having my "head in the clouds," as they say, has been a point of discussion, ongoing. But only because they can compare me to my sister. Besides looking identical, we do not have much in common where organization and time management are concerned. She is magnificent, and everything she does goes platinum. She's phenomenal.

My sister, Virginia, or Gini, is amazing. I can't deny it. And never Ginny, by the way, and for the record. She's the second-born but ended up with all firstborn traits. Go figure. I'm Claire, the firstborn—by two minutes, who acts anything but that.

As I've heard, first-borns are natural leaders, ambitious, left-brained, etc. I'm none of those things. I think I take more after my Auntie May and my grandma, Ivy, except more subdued. Those two are wild and colorful characters!

My grandma's advice for losing weight is to "suck a potato chip until you forget you're hungry." I don't quite understand that, but I do know to walk away quickly in public whenever she busts out some disco-era dance moves. She's darling at embarrassing anyone close by.

Then there is Auntie May, who is unapologetically opinionated and bold. I mean, who just up and buys a haunted Scottish castle for art students to study in? But enough of all that. I've been dying to read this book. It's supposed to be a riveting romance with some supernatural twists. Or is it a riveting supernatural tale with some romantic twists? Anyway . . .

I stared at the cover. *DIORVAL* was written in silver against a black background. I opened it and got a whiff of that new book smell. I dove right in. The idea that it was based on true events tickled my curiosity.

EXCERPT FROM DIORVAL

During my studies abroad in Scotland, I fell in love with two men. The first was a fellow art student, who I married two years later. I knew right away that I would marry Ben, my compadre in art, because we had almost everything in common. We were like peas and carrots. We loved the same food, laughed at the same humor, and sketched similar subject matter.

Ben and I found out "we" were pregnant in the new millennium. It was a big deal for our families and for us too, of course. We were married, settled, and putting down roots in a meaningful way. Both of us had sown our wild oats, and we were ready to be "grown up." A baby would augment our love and our life together.

I knew all of Ben's quirks. How the hair on the left side of his head always tufted up first thing in the morning and needed to be tamed to a respectable style. I also knew that he had wet the bed as a child until he was ten years old. Not to mention, there were many stories his siblings had laughed about from childhood concerning his fears, his tendency to be a know-it-all and a snitch, as well as all the silly and stupid antics he had been part of while growing up.

Siblings were good for this come-to-Jesus, tell-all of each other. Not ever of themselves, apparently. I wouldn't know about that, though, as I had been an only child.

He also knew all my embarrassing and shameful habits and experiences of childhood and adolescence. He'd seen pictures of my terrible haircuts and, furthermore, ridiculous hairstyles. Not to mention my faulty fashion choices. He'd learned of my obsessions, compulsions, and sensitivities. Yes, I was a chronic nail biter and often would double check, even triple check things—like doors being locked and lights turned off. Ben had grown to accept these enduring oddities about me and after a short time, seemed to get sucked into my realm, where it all seemed normal.

As far as my sensitivities went, he witnessed those right off the bat. In fact, it was before we officially started dating.

You could say that my interest in art may have pulled me away from my true calling. I maybe could have been a gifted mystic, clairvoyant, or even a psychic. I say this because on an almost daily basis, I have seen, heard, and conversed with ghosts—or spirits, as some say.

I often think back about how Ben could've written me off as a head case when he first experienced my otherworldly encounters back in Scotland all those years ago. But he was open-minded enough, or I was cute enough, for him to embrace this unique quality of mine. I guess his acceptance of weird, creepy me is what made me fall head over heels for him.

The other man I mentioned earlier is quite a different story. Perhaps, unattainable would be the best way to describe him. A sort of lost soul. Because of those qualities, I still thought of him often. Truth be told, he had crawled into my heart, and I couldn't remove him.

He would remain forever in Scotland. And I would never see him again. Now that I was pregnant, I thought of him almost constantly and remembered the stories he'd told me. I especially remembered the one about his late wife. It never stopped haunting me . . .

I awoke to the clamors of three drunken college women and Joy.

"He's such a loser!" Julie tossed her purse onto the nearby bed.

Carissa's giggling melted into an onslaught of hiccups, which handily pacified her.

"I think he's nice," Joy said shyly.

"Nice for a douche," Tiffany added.

"Who are you guys talking about?" I asked, sitting up in bed. My book fell to the floor with a thud. I had fallen asleep with the light on.

Julie shot me a look before turning her back to me. She rummaged through her bag, still not answering my question.

Tiffany answered quickly, "Vic."

"I think he's nice," Joy said again, looking at me.

"OK," I said, adding, "I've never really talked to him."

"Anyway," Julie spouted again, "That pub was lame, but it's the only place to go unless we drink here at the castle."

Tiffany belched suddenly and covered her mouth in apparent embarrassment.

Joy giggled as I looked on.

"Did you guys have fun?" I asked.

"I had fun," Joy answered. Carissa nodded in agreement.

"How far was the walk?" I wondered aloud.

"Far enough for me," Tiffany admitted, seeming to break the silent allegiance with Julie, who avoided me.

"It was kind of a spooky walk back," Joy said, taking a seat at the end of my bed.

I leaned toward her. "How so?"

She took a moment, seeming to carefully gather her thoughts. "It's like the wind is alive."

A chill ran through me, leaving goosebumps in its wake. "Why do you say that?"

Joy shrugged. "I've just never heard anything like it before. The intensity of it changes in different places."

"Really?"

Tiffany suddenly asked, "Didn't it seem more windy on the footbridge?"

"Yes," Joy said, her face brightening for a moment. "And the howling sounded different too."

"Everything is haunted around here," Julie said with a seemingly bored resignation to the possibility of "hauntedness."

"I'm actually reading a book about that," I said.

"Are you sure that's a good idea?" Julie's voice was shrill, insistent. "Don't you think you'll be too much in your head now?"

"I'm always in my head."

"Me too," Joy said quietly.

I smiled at her, feeling an undeniable vulnerability from her.

I rubbed my eyes, fighting a yawn and said, "We should probably go to bed. We have orientation in the morning."

"True," Joy agreed.

"Oh, wow. The high schooler is responsible," Julie commented with a snicker.

I shrugged. "I've always been an old soul."

My comment dropped as everyone readied themselves for bed.

I fell asleep, thinking about the wind and what Joy said. She and I thought so similarly, it seemed. Just the idea that the wind could be "alive." I thought how she and I would probably be friends.

Something woke me up a few hours later. An icy chill entered the bedroom, touched my face, and lingered above me before settling next to me. I pulled my covers up tightly under my chin. The heavy blankets pinned me snugly to the mattress.

I drifted back to sleep, half-convinced that someone was whispering, "Hello, my love. Hello, Claire."

CHAPTER TWO

Kaya

A ren't you glad I talked you two into this?" Livy stretched her legs in front of her. Her feet nearly touched the white sand, coming up a few inches shy.

Kaya peeked from under her floppy hat to observe her sister's flawless style: tanned legs glowing in the sun, perfectly fitting red and white polka dot suit, and complementary polka-dotted beach towel. Fabulous, as usual.

"Yeah, it's pretty good," May said between bites of biscotti.

"You're getting crumbs everywhere!" Livy said, brushing her hands together over the sand.

"Oh, help yourself. I'm sure that tastes exactly like the part I'm eating," May said.

"Lord, help me. What's wrong with you?" Livy asked. "Who eats biscotti on the beach? It's like eighty degrees out here."

"I do. Duh." May shrugged. Her bright orange muumuu and matching hat fit the beach scene well.

"I should always sit between you two," Kaya said, taking the floppy hat from over her face and sitting up before placing it atop her head.

"Is Cole coming out at all today?" Livy asked, lowering her sunglasses.

"Hopefully, he feels better soon," Kaya said.

"Well, he's not a spring chicken anymore. None of us are. I wouldn't trust that much seafood on one platter anywhere. The odds were against him from the start," May said.

"And Nigel's not joining us?" Kaya asked, grabbing the condensation-laden glass from its stronghold in the sand. She sipped, keeping eye contact with Livy.

"Your darling brother-in-law doesn't do well in the sun," Livy said, grabbing her drink. She took a swallow, then finished her thought, "Gets as red as a lobster, as you know."

"I do know that. Yes. And another yes to your earlier question. I'm glad you insisted upon this vacation. I've wanted to come back here for ages. Luc and I traveled through Italy when we were first married, but we never stayed on the Mediterranean." Kaya's gaze drifted toward the sea. Luc had been her second husband—a relationship full of passion, promises, and, eventually, pain. Grieving him had been complicated, not just because he was gone, but because of everything unresolved when he passed.

"Ah, this water." Livy sighed.

Kaya gazed out upon the smooth, cool aquamarine in all its languid beauty. She felt a calm take over her body. Exhaling deeply, she agreed with Livy, "Yes."

"I mean, look at the different hues of blue out there. There's like sea-foam green and every blue in between until you hit the sapphire and cobalt tones." Livy spoke in a dreamy voice.

May took off her hat and mussed her silver hair into a frenzy of waves.

"I really like you with your natural color," Kaya said to May.

"Thank you. How long are you two going to keep dumping chemicals on your heads?" May asked.

"Forever," Livy said, lying back again and lowering her shades over her eyes.

"You'll have to pry the bleach bottle from my cold, dead hands," Kaya said, smiling.

"I admire your *au naturel* thing, May," Livy said.

"Well, it's free, and I don't care," May said. "I've never cared about looking pretty."

"Yet you have always been pretty." Kaya smiled again.

"Aww," May said before stuffing the remainder of biscotti in her mouth.

"How old are you, Kiki?" Livy asked, turning her head.

Kaya laughed. "I'm a year older than you."

"OK, but how old am I?" Livy asked while breaking into a giggle, the mature timbre of her voice audible.

"I knew it!" May said.

"Knew what?" Livy asked.

"Just that. You've been going through life not knowing how old you are."

"That's why she always looks fabulous," Kaya said.

"You literally just turned fifty-nine," May said, rolling her eyes before tugging her hat down over her ears.

"I don't feel that old. My trips are in college, though, so I must be. Can you believe it?" Livy asked. "Those three little ladies are going to set the world on fire."

"Where did the time go?" Kaya wondered aloud. The sun blazed, sending a heat wave through the air.

"How is Claire liking her stay at my castle?" May asked.

Kaya shifted. "I haven't heard from her since the day she arrived. I'm trying to give her space. She wants independence, you know. And it's time for her to start launching. Cole needs a tranquilizer to sleep. He worries about the twins whenever they're gone too far or too long."

"Nigel is exactly like that too," Livy said. "What is Gini up to?"

"She's taking college courses this summer. Like Claire, but not art and not abroad."

"Genius really is in our blood, isn't it?" May stated more than asked. She glanced around. "Is our waiter coming back? I'm running low on vermouth."

"Someone's not messing around," Livy commented.

"It's my vacation, dude." May held up her glass while looking toward the bar. She clinked the remaining ice cubes around, giving an insistent glare at the bartender.

Her energy apparently jolted the bartender, as he gave a jump and grabbed his tray before rushing toward her.

"Martini Rosso on the rocks, *per favore*," May ordered.

He scribbled on his notepad and looked toward Kaya with eyebrows raised.

"Ice water, *prego*," Kaya said.

"Same," Livy said. "*Prego.*"

The beach pulsed with sunbathers and swimmers. Striped umbrellas of yellow, blue, coral, and green lined the shore of the beach, shading both tourists and locals as they soaked in persistent sun rays.

Kaya noticed the beach had been steadily filling up with locals. The Italian tradition was to take a siesta after lunch, resume the workday later in the afternoon, and then enjoy nightlife until the wee hours. Kaya reveled in the carefree, casual vibe of this coastal town with its narrow, cobblestone streets, old brick and terra cotta buildings, and ample places to eat and drink outdoors while admiring seaside vistas.

Checking her phone, Kaya saw nothing new from either of her daughters. She told herself to stop worrying. While they would always be her babies—indeed, the babies she thought she'd never have—they were almost young adults now, and she'd have to get used to these times when they were away, living their lives. It was admittedly a hard adjustment.

She glanced at Livy, who was apparently snoozing now. Kaya wanted to pick her sister's brain about how best to cope with this transition of her girls growing up and detaching.

"You OK, Kiki?" May asked.

Kaya snapped out of her trance and forced a smile. "Yeah, just thinking."

"Are you worried about Claire?"

"A little," Kaya admitted.

"Her first big trip alone."

"Exactly."

"She's going to be fine. The housemother is the granny type, very nurturing and protective. A little dramatic, but that goes with the territory. Try to relax and enjoy your vacation. You did your job as a mom. You raised two brilliant, beautiful, good-hearted daughters. They are supposed to go into the world and share what you taught them."

"That's really beautiful, May."

She shrugged. "Once in a while."

"You're right. Everything will be OK. Just keep breathing and enjoy life as it happens."

Livy stirred from her slumber and wiped the corner of her mouth before asking, "Was I snoring?"

Kaya chuckled. "No, just a little drooling."

Livy smiled. "I can live with that."

The waiter arrived with icy drinks. Clinking of ice cubes against glass preceded his delivery.

"What are your girls doing this summer?" Kaya asked Livy.

"Oh, I don't know for sure. They could tell me anything, and I'd believe them. They're renting a house off campus this year, so imagine these three identical beauties and all the fun they could be having. I think Holly is mostly working. Heather and Hazel are taking summer courses and working."

"They are good girls," May said.

"We were too, though—mostly," Kaya said.

"I mean, I was smoking a lot of weed and doing mushrooms, but my intentions were good." May laughed.

"That stuff was illegal back then. That's so crazy," Livy mused.

"Why do you think I was doing it?" May asked, her tone playful.

"A rebel all day," Kaya said with a smile.

"I paid my dues and served my consequences," May said.

"You were so hilarious in high school. When you wore that garbage bag . . ." Livy's words faded into a giggle.

"And the bone hanging on hemp twine around your neck," Kaya reminded.

"I was making statements about various issues," May said. "And no wonder I had a lot of dogs following me around. Literally. They wanted that bone."

The three sisters howled in laughter, long enough to attract the inquisitive looks of a few fellow beachgoers.

"What was the garbage bag about?" Livy asked.

"Well, the kids in my class were so obsessed with brand-name clothes and so judgmental toward kids whose parents couldn't afford them. I wanted to prove that being cool had nothing to do with what you wear."

"Did the message get across to everyone?" Kaya asked.

"No. They were dumb kids. We all were. But they did think I was cool for wearing a garbage bag." May took a long swig of vermouth, emptying her glass. "Dip shits."

Kaya brushed a strand of hair away from her eyes, shaking with laughter as a refreshing breeze wafted through. A singular cloud danced over the sun while more clouds gathered in the distance.

"Well, Ladies, I'm going to check on my dear husband and give in to my urges to be a helicopter parent," Kaya announced, gathering her beach bag and towel. "I shouldn't worry, but I do." Kaya stood with her beach bag over one shoulder and towel draped over the other.

"Your girls are smart and strong," May reminded with a gentle look Kaya's way.

"Right," Kaya said. "It's the rest of the world that concerns me."

"See you at dinner?" Livy asked.

"Of course. *Ciao.*" Kaya winked and turned on her heel toward the cliffside hotel.

Claire's silence was not sitting right with Kaya. She wouldn't relax until she talked with her again. Kaya just had a gut feeling about her older daughter. And her intuition was usually right.

CHAPTER THREE

Claire

My paintbrush glided over the canvas smoothly. Another still life of flowers. That was my favorite subject to paint. That or I was just stuck. No. It was my favorite.

While dipping my brush into the puddle of blue paint, the image of my mother flooded my mind. Curious. She was probably worrying because we hadn't had a real conversation beyond my quick check-in from the plane, but I wasn't sure what to tell her. I imagined that much of what I might describe to her would further worry her, so I was still formulating a good summation that might ease her mind.

I didn't want to tell her how spooky the wind sounded, that my roommates had drinking on the brain most of the time, or that supervision was extremely scarce. *Or* that the castle definitely felt haunted. So, what would that leave?

I guessed I could tell her how kind our housemother was and how I liked the art professor, Ms. Haas, who guided us through orientation this morning. She seemed like a lovely, knowledgeable lady. I could also tell her about Joy.

The art studio was empty. My cohort was elsewhere. I swiped through my contacts and pressed on "Mom."

My mom answered on the first ring, her voice eager, "Claire! I'm so glad you called."

"Hi, Mom. Sorry, it took me a bit. I've been jet-lagged. You know how that is. Did you make it to your little Italian village?" I asked, wanting to shift focus off me as much as possible.

"Yes. We drove down from Rome last night."

"All of you in one vehicle?" I asked.

"Yep, it was an interesting car ride," Mom explained.

I chuckled. "It can't not be interesting with my aunties riding together."

"Exactly. Throwing your uncle and dad in the mix is the icing on top."

"How many times did Auntie May need to stop?"

"Like six or seven."

"That must have driven Uncle Nigel nuts," I surmised.

"Close, but she shared her snacks with him, so he kept it together."

I laughed, picturing my motley crew of a family traveling through Italy. They would stand out so obviously as Americans. Well, Uncle Nigel is technically a Brit, but . . .

I sighed and said, "I'm sorry we didn't really talk sooner, Mom. I know how you worry. I was just wiped out." Half-truth.

Mom returned my sigh. "It's OK as long as you're OK."

"Thanks, Mom. I am OK. Are you guys having fun?"

"Yes, we girls were just on the beach."

"Must be hot there, huh?"

"Yeah, like eighties."

"Auntie May tossing back sweet vermouth?"

"Like a champ."

"Sounds nice. It's cold, rainy, and windy here."

"That's too bad. How's castle living? How are your roommates?"

"Uh, the castle is drafty and musty smelling but awesomely old and interesting. Everything is made from stone. I mean, not everything. You know—all the structural elements."

"I do. And your roommates, are they treating you all right?"

"Oh, yeah. All is good." Another half-truth.

"Good."

"Will you guys have dinner on a boat in the Mediterranean or something cool?"

"I hope not. I like land. You know how seasick I get."

"True, Mom."

"What are your dinner plans for tonight?"

"Our housemother is cooking."

"That could be adventurous."

"I can't remember what she's making tonight."

"Hopefully, not cow stomach."

"Ew, is that really a thing?" My stomach dipped.

"Unfortunately, yes. And don't count out the possibility of sheep lungs," Mom teased.

"If those things show up on the menu, I'll go on a diet while I'm here," I half-joked. Though, the thought of what my mother had just mentioned as dinner possibilities seriously made any appetite I may have had disappear for the moment. "Well, anyway, I'm jealous of you guys. I'm sure there is seafood galore on the menu where you are tonight."

"Definitely. Your father went overboard on it last night and has been recovering all day."

"Sheesh, that's no fun. Tell Dad I hope he feels better soon and that I love him."

"I will, honey."

"I love you too, of course. Will you give everyone hugs for me and tell Auntie May that I love her castle too?"

"Of course, sweetheart. I love you too."

"OK. Talk soon."

"Yes, love. Stay warm and safe."

"Will do, Mom. Have fun."

"Bye."

"Goodbye."

I ended the call and made the final strokes on my painting for the day. Carrying my brushes to the sink, I paused at the window and watched the wind have its way with the tall grasses. A chill crept through me as I focused on the sound of the howling wind. Relentless. I wondered then if the sunny days here were creepy as well.

The door creaked as Joy meandered into the room, her backpack slung over her shoulder.

She smiled and greeted me, "Hi, Claire. Mind if I join you?"

"Oh, come right in. I'm just finishing up."

Her flushed face was nearly as pink as the wool sweater she wore.

"Are you OK?" I asked.

She fumbled with the strap of her backpack as she set it on the table.

Looking down, she answered, "Yeah. Are you all right?"

I nodded, not believing her, though I pursued it no further. At the sink, I let warm water run over my brush bristles as the blue, green, red, and orange hues faded into a watery, brownish-gray swirl and disappeared down the drain. The gentle lapping of water lulled me into a trance.

"Claire?" Joy's voice brought me back to reality.

"Sorry. I was daydreaming." I blushed with my admission.

"It's OK. I was just wondering something."

"For sure."

"Did you hear anything strange last night?" Joy whispered.

My eyes scanned the room, searching for the reason she might be whispering. We were alone, so it didn't make any sense to me.

"What do you mean?" I asked, feeling my pulse pick up a bit.

"Like someone talking." she said.

The hair on the back of my neck shot up. I knew what she meant. I'd heard someone say my name. However, I did not want to feed into her apparent fear. It didn't seem like an OK thing to do.

"It was probably the guys. Their room is just over there." I pointed at the wall to my right.

"But wouldn't we hear them all the time?"

Yeah, and the walls are solid stone, I thought to myself.

I grasped at a probable explanation. "Well, we've all heard the story that the castle is likely haunted. They were probably at our door, messing with us. You know, Vic has the reputation for being a joker."

She nodded slowly in seeming agreement, but I could see in her eyes that she was not having my explanation.

Joy's chest rose and fell with a deep breath as she half-sighed, "OK. You're probably right. I won't worry about it. I'm sure Effie was probably exaggerating too—just to cause a buzz."

I studied her for a moment. Her porcelain skin luminated in its flawless glow. Green eyes, large and bright, sparkled even at this moment of uncertainty. Her smooth, shiny, auburn hair boasted a chic pixie cut. Small diamond studs glimmered from her earlobes. She was quiet, reserved, and refined. The depths of her heart shone whenever she smiled. I imagined that she had likely endured the onslaught of bullies in her childhood and maybe even still. And for no reason other than her kindness, which she did not hesitate to show or give.

Joy lacked the edge that was needed to deter the likes of a mean-hearted person. Her peaceful vibe was certain to irritate a spiteful, unhappy soul, and the resulting envy would transform her into a target.

I felt myself soften to her yet again. I imagined how her shyness was probably a result of her past dealings with jerks and assholes. I also imagined for a moment how she'd been very loved as a young girl. Her parents likely encouraged her creativity and free-spiritedness. Maybe she had even grown very confident in her artistic creativity.

And then, she would go to school and encounter the many types and levels of other children, many of whom were deeply unhappy. I knew this because I'd experienced it too. Except, I had always fought back. Not physically, but intellectually. I can't account for how I gained this edge, but judging from my mom's moxie and my aunties' humor as well as gall, I tacked it up to heredity. And for that, I was grateful. Maybe even the unconscious competition with my twin sister had something to do with it. Steel sharpens steel, after all.

I added something then, not to be condescending, rude, or thought-less, but because I truly believed it. "Besides, if there is a ghost, we'll just make peace with it. Just listen and explain that we're just visiting, and we'll be respectful."

She stared at me as though I were insane.

After a few moments, she asked, "And you're sure he'll listen?"

Now, it was my turn to stare. It was her knowing confidence in the fact that the ghost in question was a "he."

It had definitely been a male's voice saying my name the other night. A shiver eddied through me.

CHAPTER FOUR

EXCERPT FROM DIORVAL

My first encounter with him was terrifying, not because he was inherently frightening, but because of the unnerving urgency in his voice that enveloped me like a suffocating fog. His accent was thick, the syllables tumbling out in a rhythm that danced just out of reach of my understanding. And there he was—his translucent form flickering in the dim light, sitting beside my bed in the dead of night, a ghost wrapped in shadows and secrets. The air around us crackled with an electric tension, a silent promise of something ancient and forbidden.

But the worst part, the most unsettling truth, was the growing doubt gnawing at my mind. Was this real, or was I spiraling into madness? Who would believe me, anyway? A ghost, a grave truth wrapped in layers of disbelief, whispering secrets of the past—what could I possibly say to make anyone understand? The clock ticked on, each chime echoing my isolation as I wrestled with the choice to unravel the mystery, even from myself.

CHAPTER FIVE

Kaya

Cole squeezed Kaya's hand as they sauntered through the narrow, cobblestone alley.

"Where should we get lunch today?" he asked.

Kaya looked up at her husband and the crinkles at the edges of his eyes, knowing that she had similar lines on her face. He had taken to shaving his head years ago. Maybe it was a bit of vanity because he didn't want to be gray, but she was on her own campaign in that way too, at least for now. She admitted that it was a funny thing to hold on to, but it gave her a sense of control, however small.

With her girls growing up so fast, she felt that imaginary stronghold on her youth ever slipping out of reach. And by youth, she meant her former middle-aged status. There was humor in there somewhere. She mused for a moment about the chapters of letting go that life kept presenting. Every time she thought that she really understood, another layer was revealed.

Kaya yanked herself back to the present moment. She was standing in a narrow alleyway in beautiful Italy with her beloved husband, searching for a picturesque place to eat lunch. This was like a dream, and thanks to the lessons of many earlier chapters, she knew she needed to live fully in this moment.

She leaned into Cole, popping up on her tiptoes to graze his cheek with her lips.

He smiled and pulled her into his arms, capturing her mouth with his. His kiss transported her through the myriad emotions that only he could evoke from her. The tenderness interwoven with passion, the excitement securely tethered to familiar warmth, all melting together into joyful satisfaction.

Her heart fluttered as he moved his lips to her forehead and gave her another squeeze before staring into her eyes. She couldn't count the number of times his eyes had twinkled at hers in the last seventeen years.

"I think I want gnocchi," Kaya finally answered her husband's question.

"That does sound good." He smiled in agreement.

"Let's find the most breath-taking view," Kaya said.

"Deal." Cole grabbed her hand and forged ahead.

They took a seat on a patio overlooking the sea. The air filled Kaya's lungs with anticipation and glee. Under the red umbrella, they were sheltered from the midday sun, which ascended to its zenith above them. Hanging plants, filled with lush greens, fuchsia, red, and yellow flowers and flowing vines canopied around them.

They admired the sea, tearing their eyes away only to steal a glance at one another. Cole's satisfied grin warmed Kaya's heart. She never stopped being grateful for him, for his love, his kindness and devotion. He was so many things to her: her confidante, love, husband, father of her children, her heart. Joyful overwhelm filled her being every time she realized how he had blessed her life.

The waiter arrived, took their drink orders, and disappeared just as quickly as he'd arrived. A breeze blew in from the sea, and Kaya breathed a deeply contented sigh.

Cole grabbed his wife's hand and poured a heart-melting gaze into her blue-gray eyes. "Kaya Boucher, you have made my life the most beautiful work of art. From the day I met you up until this moment, you have never stopped exciting me. I always look forward to whatever is next for us. Our life is an amazing and wonderful adventure because of you. Everything you do is dream-quality. If you only knew how many times I've stopped to pinch myself over the last seventeen years."

Kaya's eyes brimmed with tears at this unexpected litany of praise and appreciation. She squeezed Cole's hand before bringing it up to her lips, placing a kiss in his palm.

"Thank you for loving me through everything. I have always felt so blessed to have found you. You are the love of my life," Kaya said quietly yet firmly.

Cole stared, apparently breathing in her presence. The time seemed to fly by more quickly each day. Kaya wondered, how many smiles had they shared over the years? It seemed to Kaya that Cole had made it his mission ever since they'd taken vows as husband and wife to see to it that more tears of joy than sorrow ever rolled down Kaya's face.

"I feel the same. We are blessed, and I love you more with each day," Cole said, pulling her hand in for a kiss.

The waiter interrupted their tender moment, bringing their drinks and standing ready to take their lunch order.

Moments later, Cole said, "Babe, I hope you're able to enjoy this getaway a little more, now that you've heard from the girls."

Kaya shifted in her seat, feeling appreciative of her husband's deep knowing of her. He'd witnessed her worry about their daughters count-less times, and always, he was the voice of calm and reason. He balanced her anxiety and worry in the most natural way.

"I think so," she said with a nod, setting down her water glass. "I have to let go and let life happen. And funny thing, I thought I had already figured out how to do that. I guess having kids does something to that."

"Well said, my love," Cole agreed.

"I never thought I would have two such beautiful, brilliant daugh-ters, and it's been a challenge not to be one of those overbearing mothers. I hope I've succeeded in letting them have their freedom and room to grow."

"You have, my dear," Cole reassured. "I'm guilty of overthinking and worrying about them too."

Kaya laughed. "You hide it better than me. You're always the cool dad. This trip is actually the only time I've noticed any obvious worry from you."

Cole gave a wayward glance toward the water for a moment before responding, "Claire is so sensitive. I can't help but hope that her classmates are kind. She's a threat, being that her level of talent is exceptional. But I know she's tough like her mother and can handle herself."

Kaya nodded. "She's gotten through some rough situations on her own."

"True."

"I could worry myself sick, I know. So, I'm going to think peaceful, positive thoughts and wait for her to reach out."

"Good plan, love." Cole held up his drink to Kaya, and they clinked glasses.

CHAPTER SIX

Claire

D inner surprised me with how delicious and satisfying it was. Lamb, again, but yum! We were in the old country, after all. The land of meat and potatoes. I loved the mushrooms and sauce Effie had whipped up. She was an incredible cook.

With my belly full, I wanted nothing more than to relax, all snuggled in my cozy bed, and do some light reading. My cohort had buzzed about playing some board games, and I picked up on the detail that they were going to drink as well. So, a drinking game was essentially about to happen. I had no such interest. Thank goodness I was "too young." They mostly respected that fact. Only Julie commented under her breath when I declined their onslaught about participating.

Once everyone left the room, I switched off the lamp at my bedside and gave a small chuckle at the radio alarm clock next to the lamp. My dad had one similar on his nightstand back home. My sister and have I always teased him about keeping outdated things like that. I missed my parents for a moment and fought the feeling of being alone.

Alone, except for the wind that seemed to always howl and sometimes scream at night. I supposed being so close to the sea had something to do with it.

There in the darkness, I felt for my clip-on reading light in the mass of blankets. A remnant of my mother's voice jostled through my head with her consistently friendly reminder about being organized. A smile crept over my expression as I thought of her.

I was so lucky to have my parents. They remained over-protective, and now that I was older, I really appreciated that. I thought of my sister, Gini, too. She was loving as well. She didn't try to compete. She was just naturally good at everything. That had been a frustrating fact of life for me in my younger years, but I was learning to embrace it. We were identical but different too. She was amazing at everything, but I was pretty good at art. I was learning to feel proud of myself and stop comparing. But it was challenging.

While my twin was getting a crazy number of likes on social media for her compelling words or heroic deeds, I was perched at my easel, being . . . well . . . boring.

Her life and lifestyle didn't interest me. It didn't feel true or deep to me. Old soul. That's what people kept referring to me as.

Gini also always had a boyfriend and was always in love. I'd had one boyfriend and wasn't sure how I'd felt, really.

I remember how I'd told my mom that I wasn't sure if love was in my future, and she told me that I was too young to know that for sure. Mom said to focus on school, plan to travel, and trust that everything would work out the way it's supposed to. She'd always add, with a sparkle in her eyes, "Plan to be surprised." She reminded me that Gini and I had been the best surprise of her life. Along with meeting my dad too, of course.

I found the small light and clipped it to the top of the page with the dog-eared marking. The page glowed under the illumination instantly. The words were not absorbing, as hard as I tried to concentrate. The darkness of the room settled onto me and pressed down around the edges of my blankets, effectively tucking me in. My body radiated a cozy warmth, but my face registered the damp coolness of the room.

Mustiness lingered in the air, assaulting my olfactory sensitivities. The faint aroma of moth balls topped off the odoriferous menagerie of smells. Thankfully, both were subtle, or I knew I wouldn't be able to sleep. I happily pressed my lavender-scented tissue to my nose. After breathing deeply a few times, my body relaxed, and my mind quickly followed.

Focusing again on the book, I let my imagination form pictures as I read. Soon, I was in that place between dream and reality. Very relaxed—almost deliriously so.

In a dreamscape, I ran through a field of white flowers. Glancing down at myself, I noticed that I was wearing a white, lacy dress. Then, someone took my hand. I turned to see a handsome boy running beside me. He smiled, his eyes twinkling as his dimples deepened. His dark hair, thick and wavy, reminded me of a time long passed.

Looking into his eyes, I felt something inside myself soften and go fluid. Something inside me broke free. Heat built up behind my eyes, tears gathering suddenly. My smile faded as curiosity took hold. We stopped running and stood face-to-face, breathlessly staring into each other's eyes. My heart pounded as I watched myriad emotions play out in his eyes and secrets, ancient and lost in some faraway time.

A new world seemed to open with a force so powerful, my very center grew heavy, as though the weight of centuries could transpire in a single moment. He squeezed my hand, and time blurred. I felt myself quaking inside, stuck somewhere between bliss and panic, as though I may lose myself.

I jerked back to reality, the realness of his touch lingering on my skin. Hastily, I sat up, heart racing, and flipped my bedside lamp on. What had I just experienced? It felt like more than a dream.

My heart light and head buzzing, I felt electrified. The image of his smile burned in my mind. White teeth, dimples, the gleam in his eyes. Not to mention, the fervor with which he squeezed my hand.

A flurry of activity burst through the door just then as my cohort returned from their latest drinking episode.

Julie cackled loudly as she barged through the threshold, the others in tow. Her glossy eyes revealed obvious alcohol consumption. Furthermore, her loud voice and brash words bordered on abusive.

"Oh, Joy," Julie started brazenly, "you obviously were home-schooled. You're too nice and innocent. I'll help you find your way out of your shell. You're so naïve."

The others looked on quietly as Joy appeared near tears. Her chin trembled as she put her head down and moved quickly to her chest of drawers. She rummaged through the top drawer.

Then, I saw the tears streaming silently down her cheeks.

"Leave her alone!" The words burst from me before I had the chance to choose them.

Julie's eyes narrowed as they slid in my direction. She laughed before sneering, "I'm sure Baby has an opinion about everything. Your silver spoon is showing."

Joy had turned and stared silently at me, apparently trying to hide that she was wiping away tears.

I cleared my throat and replied, "I do have an opinion about this."

Julie mocked me, repeating my words in a snide tone and wiggling her head while making hand gestures.

I felt hotness building in my chest and climbing into my throat—a wave of nausea hitting me. I hated confrontation, but I hated bullying more.

Joy, suddenly at my side, patted my arm. "It's OK, Claire."

"Is it?" Julie asked her features contorted in what appeared to be anger. "Is it OK, Joy?"

My face flushed instantaneously, my chest tightening and heart racing. My palms suddenly sweaty, I wiped them on my pajama bottoms and swung my legs over the side, ready to catapult to my feet.

I feared what I might say next. Head down, I forced a deep inhale, not wanting to do something I'd later regret.

"Cat got your tongue, Baby?" Julie pressed me. Her face had taken on a serpentine quality.

"My name is Claire," I said in a low voice, looking up at her through my lashes.

I'm not sure if it was my voice or my body language that dissuaded her ongoing pursuit, but she abruptly dropped the subject. A collective sigh of relief seemed to emanate within the four walls.

Joy wiped her face again and went on rummaging through the drawers, tension hanging thick in the room and dread lingering in my heart. Another bully. Would there ever be an end to them?

CHAPTER SEVEN

Claire

This professor was different. He was American, but besides that, he had a different vibe that I couldn't explain. From the moment he entered the room, the atmosphere shifted ominously. Our orientation the other day had been led by such a kind, talented lady that I was excited and enthusiastic about the coming semester.

Now, a sense of dread crept in as this short, stout, bald man with a ridiculously large black mustache strutted about the front of the room with his belly protruding over his belt. His eyes skimmed over our group in one bored and disgusted sweep, sending a shiver down my spine. It took me a minute to recognize where I'd seen him before, and once I put it together, I had to suppress a giggle, which threatened to erupt from me. He scarily resembled a Dr. Suess character.

I must have been smiling unaware because his eyes narrowed at me, and he strode over to me, placed both palms on my table, and cleared his throat loudly while delivering a look to me that nearly seared my eyebrows.

I instantly sat up straighter and nervously adjusted the materials in front of me.

"Mizz Boucher," he whined. "Please share with your cohort what it is that you find so humorous."

He leaned on the table in a flamboyant pose with one hand on his hip, eyes gazing upward. His index finger tapped insistently on the white tabletop.

I cleared my throat and looked down, not knowing what to say. The heat rose inside me, causing my face to flush. I heard whispering from the back of the room. Most likely Julie. The burning in my cheeks intensified. My palms wet, I continued fidgeting. I didn't know how to answer his question. Even his name was funny—Professor Stump. Maybe his first name was Woody or Harry. Maybe his friends called him Tiny, or his nickname was Slim.

He cleared his throat loudly. "Well?"

I met his gaze and responded quietly, "I don't know what you mean."

Exhaling loudly, he smirked. "Are you telling me you don't know the definition of humorous? Or are you telling me that you're not in control of what your face does?"

His voice echoed in the silent room.

"No, Sir," I answered.

"Which one?" he insisted, pounding his fist on the table.

"Neither," I stammered.

He leaned in so close, his hot breath reeking of stale coffee and halitosis. I fought my own gag reflex while unable to disguise my grimace.

"I'm going to make an example of you," he whispered, his icy blue eyes shooting his threat straight into my skull. "You're the gifted one, aren't you?"

I stared at him silently.

His eyes quietly challenged me for what felt like an eternity.

I squirmed under his scrutiny.

"Gifted," he scoffed, knocking my sketch pad onto the floor with the slap of his hand. "We'll see about that."

Without missing a beat, he began describing the first project that we would be graded on.

I wiped the unexpected tears that gathered in my eyes and felt myself slowly cool down despite my pulse hammering erratically in my neck.

My shirt clung to my sweaty armpits. I felt disgusting and awkward. I wanted to run to the bedroom and crawl under my covers. Leaning over, I grabbed my sketch pad from the dusty floor.

I couldn't hear a word he said for the remainder of his class period. I kept my head down and pretended to take notes, fighting tears all the while.

When class ended, I made a beeline to the door and a mad dash toward our sleeping quarters.

Barry caught up to me halfway down the hallway.

"That dude was a straight-up dick to you, Claire," he said.

"I hadn't noticed," I tried to joke but ended up sounding sarcastic.

Joy appeared on my left. "Are you OK?" she asked.

I nodded, securing my bag over my shoulder.

"He's got it in for you," Barry continued. "That sucks. Why can't he be happy to have this opportunity to shape you as an artist? Plus, he might learn something from you. I mean, we all learn from each other. I think if I had a prodigy as a student, I'd be soaking up everything they bring to the table."

"Thanks," I said, watching my own feet as I walked.

"That's so nice of you, Barry," Joy commented, looking past me to Barry.

He shrugged. "It's true."

"I think he's intimidated by you," Joy offered. "He might be worried that he can't teach you anything."

"Good point," Barry said. "What was so funny by the way?"

I stopped in my tracks, wondering if I should share my observation with them.

I sighed in a moment of hesitation. "I shouldn't say anything. It's rude or mean. Probably both."

"Well, I really want to know now." Barry chuckled.

"I really shouldn't say anything. I don't want to risk it getting back to him."

"Come on," Barry urged, giving me a nudge.

Joy's wide eyes communicated her interest in hearing my answer.

I paused a moment, wanting to gauge Barry's trustworthiness. His gray eyes held the light of sincerity while his straight, white teeth gave the illusion of wholesomeness. And yet, I decided against sharing.

"Sorry, I'm taking it to my grave," I said.

"Aw," Joy murmured her disappointment.

"Well, OK." Barry didn't push it further.

We resumed walking and reached our rooms shortly.

As Barry turned toward his room, he said, "See you at dinner."

"Sounds good," Joy and I responded in unison.

As I was about to follow Joy through the threshold of our room, I would swear I saw a man standing in the shadows at the end of the hallway.

CHAPTER EIGHT

Claire

I awoke suddenly, the room enveloped in an icy chill so intense that I imagined seeing my breath if there were any light besides the sliver shining under the door from the hallway. Adjusting the thermostat meant abandoning the warmth of my cozy bed, so I lay there, hoping for one of my roommates to do it. The dim blue light of my clock radio read 2:13 a.m.

Dinner had been a surprising delight again, the evening happily uneventful. I had come to terms with Julie and her minions' cold indifference and found myself beyond caring for the time being.

My roommates' rhythmic breathing punctuated the silence. What was missing, oddly enough, was the usual howling wind. This rare quiet felt almost sacred. I burrowed deeper into my blankets, letting my mind wander back to the dreamscape of the other night—the field, the mysterious boy. His face, the flowers, the air—all seemed purer in my memory.

As I teetered on the edge of sleep, his voice softly said, "You're beautiful, Claire. How I adore you."

A dreamy smile formed on my face as he extended his hand toward me. I stretched my hand to touch him, feeling excitement build inside my chest. As our fingers intertwined, an icy coldness shocked through my senses.

I snatched my hand back hastily, my eyes flying open as I gasped for breath. Sitting up in bed, I turned on my bedside lamp, needing to see whatever I had just touched.

Joy stirred in her bed. "Claire, are you all right?" she asked.

My heart pounding wildly, I answered, "I think so. I just had a strange dream."

I noticed the room was not cold in the way it had been only a moment earlier.

"OK," Joy said. "Do you want to leave your lamp on for a little while?"

"Maybe."

"Do you want to talk about it?" Joy asked.

"No."

"OK. Well, I hope you get some sleep."

"Thanks. I'll turn off the lamp in a minute."

"No worries."

I switched my lamp off after a few minutes, deciding that my dream had just been very vivid and there was no further explanation needed. Whatever it was that I had felt had come from my own internal workings.

Outside, the wind picked up again, howling and moaning its haunting chant. I fell asleep to the sound of the wind, and it wasn't long until I was dreaming of him again.

CHAPTER NINE

Kaya

Kaya's legs glowed a bronze tone, outstretched in front of her. Heels burrowed into the hot, white sand, she leaned back, pressing her palms into her beach towel. Not a cloud in the sky.

"You're fast," Cole's voice floated over her head.

He carried a bottle of water, his oversized towel slung over his shoulder. His skin boasted a bronzed finish as well.

"I'm soaking up this last day of vacation sun," Kaya said. The smell of coconut surrounded her like a cloud, offering a sense of tropical bliss.

"Babe, I'm proud of you," Cole started. "You've resisted calling the girls these last few days."

Kaya smiled. "Thank you. I dialed each of them a couple times but didn't put the calls through. I had imaginary conversations where they told me how great things were going. So, I'm acting 'as if' everything is swell."

"Wow." Cole returned his wife's smile. "That's impressive."

"I impressed myself," Kaya said with a laugh. "Maybe I can keep this up once we're home too."

"You got this, babe," Cole said.

"Great minds." May's voice casually drifted into the conversation as she strolled up with her beach gear. Livy and Nigel were not far behind.

Kaya beamed. "Oh, the whole family is going to take some sun back on their return trip."

Nigel splayed his beach towel out in front of him. "I have to tell my mates I spent some time on the beach, or I'll never hear the end of it. These blokes . . ." he said, rolling his eyes.

"They apparently are very competitive about grand vacations," Livy explained, positioning herself on her neatly spread towel.

"That's unique," May said before taking a bite from her pastry.

"Where did you find that?" Cole asked May, his eyes fixed on the crumbling morsel.

May finished chewing. "Pastry envy?"

"Got that right," Cole said.

"I got it in the lobby." May wiped her fingers with a small towelette that she scrounged from her beach bag.

"I've never seen pastries in the lobby," Nigel said.

"I have connections." May winked.

"How so?" Livy asked.

A few tourists waddled past, dispersing grains of sand onto Kaya's towel.

"Sheesh!" May extended narrow-eyed disapproval toward the group momentarily before explaining, "I breakfast shamed them."

Nigel laughed. "Of course you did."

"Well,"—May gathered her explanation visibly in her chest—"I told the manager that the price of our stay warranted breakfast."

"In other words, you are the only guest getting free pastries because you complained," Livy surmised.

"No, there's one other guy too," May said with a grin.

"Brilliant, love. Well done," Nigel said.

"She's a class act," Kaya said. "Mom would be proud."

"Where do you think I learned it?" May leaned back in a satisfied pose.

"Mom's life is good. Why not emulate it?" Livy said, lowering her sunglasses over her eyes before lying back on her towel.

"She definitely figured things out," Cole said. "Your mom's strong. And clever."

The striped umbrella above Kaya's head rippled with the gentle force of a breeze.

"You guys want to come with me to Monaco? I'm meeting Mom there," May said.

"Sounds lovely, but we have to get back. The kiddos at the center are waiting patiently," Kaya said.

"You guys are amazing." Nigel glanced between Kaya and Cole.

"This is the guy who keeps it going," Kaya said, playfully tugging at the hem of Cole's polo-style shirt.

"If we had more vacation to burn, we'd join you," Livy said.

"Aw, none of you have retired, huh?" May asked.

"I don't think I'll ever retire," Cole said.

"It's very rewarding," Kaya agreed. "The kiddo who inspired us in the first place graduated from college last year. He says hello whenever he visits his mom."

"Zach? That's cool," Livy said.

"Nice," May added, nodding slowly. "So, when do you guys want to head out?"

"We should get on the road for Rome in a couple hours," Nigel said.

"This trip went too fast," Kaya said.

"Don't they always?" Livy echoed.

"True," May and Kaya said in unison, followed by, "Jinx!"

Kaya giggled while May added, "Wah-wah-wah!" like a muted trombone in a comedy act.

"Anyone want one last cocktail while on the beach?" Nigel asked.

Cole shrugged. "When in Rome."

"Close enough, and yes," Kaya said with a nod and a wink. She reached over and squeezed her husband's hand.

"Yes, love," Livy chimed in.

"Got that right," May said.

"We're going to find out how good my memory is." Nigel chuckled and headed toward the beach-side bar.

"He's a good egg," Cole said, nodding toward Nigel.

"We lucked out with him," Kaya agreed.

"He's fucking fabulous." Livy beamed, watching her husband hustle through the sand.

"He's all right. I like him. For a Brit, he's not half bad," May said, pulling her hat over her eyes once fully reclined. "And thank God you got over your southern belle thing. Let 'er fly with the obscenities."

"Well, that settles it. Fuck, yeah!" Livy said, breaking into a broad smile.

Nigel returned with a bartender in tow. With cocktails dispersed, a gleeful toast of "Cheers!" arose from the vacationers.

Kaya silently fought her worries, not wanting to tarnish this joyous occasion. Never before had she wished her intuition to be wrong so badly.

CHAPTER TEN

EXCERPT FROM DIORVAL

I walked over the bridge toward the castle, a silhouette against the twilight sky. The moment my foot touched the ancient stone, the wind howled around me, a fierce whisper that felt almost sentient. If I didn't know better, I would say the wind was screaming—each gust a desperate plea, each moan laced with anguish.

It surged suddenly, as if awakened from a long slumber, pushing against me with an otherworldly force that left me breathless.

Diorval had warned me—he had spoken in hushed tones, his eyes darting as if he could see the shadows lurking just beyond the edges of reality. "This place," he had said, "is haunted beyond your comprehension." Spirits were said to roam every inch of the castle, their sorrowful wails trapped within the very walls, echoing through the corridors of time. Each blade of grass, he claimed, held sad and terrible memories, remnants of lives cut short and unfinished tales.

As I crossed the threshold, the atmosphere thickened with palpable tension that settled over me like a shroud. I could almost feel the weight of the castle's history pressing down, beckoning me to uncover its secrets, even as the wind screamed warnings in my ears.

What would I find within those shadowed halls? Would I encounter the restless souls Diorval spoke of, or was something far more sinister waiting just beyond the threshold, eager to ensnare the curious?

CHAPTER ELEVEN

Claire

The assignment disgusted me. I felt my stomach turn as Professor Stump described our objective for our capstone project. We had to make a sculpture using trash. The one rule was to not use anything that would rot. I thanked heaven for that rule. I contemplated dropping out and returning home had that detail not been specified.

I caught Barry looking my way at the end of the assignment description. I think he had seen me trying to get my gag reflex under control. He motioned a thumbs-up sign with high eyebrows. I assumed he was making sure I was OK. I returned a thumbs up, and he smiled, signaling, "OK."

Joy leaned over to me and whispered, "We're going to the pub after class. Please join us."

I pursed my lips. "Really?"

"We're just going to play Monopoly and drink. Well, I'm not going to drink."

I thought for a moment about the experience I'd had the last time I stayed in alone. I let out a pent-up breath and replied, "I don't drink."

"You don't have to. We'll be the sober ones. It's kind of fun, just to go to the village. A change of scenery and vibe, you know? I'd really like if you came along."

Her large eyes convinced me on a different level. She was lonely. I could see it. She didn't fit in with the cohort. Like me.

"OK. I'll have soda or bubbly water or whatever," I relented.

"So, we need to save our garbage each day and also steal garbage wherever we go?" Barry asked as he slid up to Joy and me after Professor Stump left the room.

"Revolting, right?" I sought confirmation of my former impression.

"Totally," Joy agreed.

"He's got a screw loose," Barry said.

"I think he's a psychopath," I added. "No one has ever looked through my soul like that."

"He's got a lizard or serpentine look about him sometimes when he's talking," Joy said.

I was surprised by her observation. She had never spoken badly about anyone before—not that I'd heard.

"True," Barry agreed and quickly pressed on. "Claire, you should come with us to the pub this afternoon. We're playing board games."

"That's what Joy said too," I replied.

His eyes gleamed. "Is that a yes?"

I smiled. "It's a maybe."

"No pressure," Joy said, playfully jabbing me in the ribs with her elbow.

"And we walk there?" I asked.

"Yes, it's not far," Barry said.

I stared at the blue and green tartan pattern rug under my feet.

"You don't have to drink," Barry added.

"I'll think about it."

"Yay!" Joy's face lit up.

I suppressed an anxious sigh and smiled at Joy instead.

The quick walk to the pub surprised me. Low and quiet for once, the wind did not chill me to my bones this time. And upon arrival, I understood the allure of this little place. The low ceiling and soft lighting invited me to stay awhile, offering a respite from the stoney, drafty feel of the castle. While the traditional décor echoed that of the castle, a warm feeling embraced me as I slid onto the leather-clad, wooden bench of the large U-shaped booth that my cohort had chosen. The eight of us snugly filled the back corner of the pub. A wrought iron pendant light fixture hung above us, casting a pale yellow glow upon us all. Over the bar, a wooden sign informed us that we were about to imbibe at Ye Malthouse.

The tartan rug jarred my senses with its bright red and green pattern. I guess I had grown accustomed to the cool and mellow look of the tartan at the castle. Admittedly, I didn't understand what all the plaid was about. Probably tradition.

I felt happy and somewhat safe, sitting on the same side of the table as Julie, with two people between us, Joy and Tiffany. Barry sat directly opposite me, giving an occasional wink, which I didn't understand.

In attempting to discern Barry's winking, I became absorbed in my thoughts. The days were very long here, not just regarding dealing with an egomaniac of a professor or dealing with Julie and her minions, but literally. This was the time of year when it remained light outside extra-long, and darkness wasn't truly dark. Effie had said just that. It's why the curtain in our bedroom was black-out quality, but even that didn't help me sleep sometimes.

Vic set down the American board game Apples to Apples. We were the only customers in the place for the moment. The barkeep had just lit a fire in the hearth. Though it had been the warmest day that I'd experienced here since arriving, it was destined to cool down as evening approached. These stone buildings were notoriously chilly as well.

A fleeting thought of my dream companion floated into my mind's eye. I wondered if he'd return tonight. My curiosity nagged at me so much so that I jumped when Joy leaned into me with a question.

"Are you OK?" Joy asked and then repeated her question. "Do you want to be on my team or Barry's?"

"Yours," I muttered numbly.

Barry jotted down everyone's drink orders on a napkin and headed to the bar after collecting a handful of our bills and coins.

I asked for a ginger ale, and Joy followed suit.

"The Stump is killing me. How about you guys?" Vic asked with a smirk, raising one eyebrow with his question. He slid into Barry's spot as he waited for an answer.

Joy and I looked at each other in silence.

Vic didn't wait for a response. He seemed ready to dive in with his opinion.

"I might go to hell for saying this, but he is the worst. He's the most egotistical professor I've experienced. Talk about a power-hungry dictator! Is he seriously going to have us piling up trash in that classroom for weeks? Can we get him fired?" He laughed with exaggerated swagger, obviously secure in his own confidence.

I nodded, feeling cautious about endorsing his comments wholeheartedly.

I noticed Joy raise her hand and rest it under her chin, the way she did when she was feeling nervous or shy.

Vic pressed, "He really has it in for you, Claire. Your genius bothers him. Have you noticed?"

"I picked up on that," I said quietly, not wanting to be the topic of any conversation, now or later.

Vic leaned in, causing the table to slide toward me and Joy. I put my palms up and held it in place.

He said slyly, "I think he's a real fuck twit, don't you?"

I shrugged. "Maybe he'll redeem himself."

"Well played," Vic said, pulling back and sliding into his original spot on the bench, gazing at me from the corner of his eye as he rubbed his index finger over his top lip.

I felt a chill run through me as an uneasy sensation settled into my stomach.

Barry returned with a tray of drinks. Setting the tray in front of Joy and me, he announced, "Time to drink up, lushes!"

Laughter arose from the table. With drinks dispersed, Barry took a seat.

Vic raised his pint high in the air. "A drink to our worst professor—Stump!"

"Boo!" Julie, Tiffany, and Barry synced their voices in a low pitch.

Joy and I held up our soda cans in momentary solidarity.

While glasses clinked, Julie added, "He's a loser!"

More laughter trundled.

Barry motioned his glass toward me. "Thanks for taking one for the team, Claire."

I half-smiled and tapped my can of ginger ale against his glass, not knowing what he meant but also not wanting to invite any more conversation that featured me as the topic.

The table grew silent except for Vic, who gave a nod. "Thanks, kid."

I took a swallow of my soda, desperately wanting the topic of conversation to change, as I toyed with the diamond bracelet on my wrist.

Joy whispered, "We should bring our cans back with us."

I smiled at her in agreement, holding my breath for Julie to chime in with a sarcastic comment about me. To my surprise, she refrained.

We played a few rounds of the game, and I actually had fun. My cohort was not shy about their alcohol consumption, and I wondered if it was just a rite of passage or if this was how they dealt with the pressure of school and being away from home. I am guilty of overthinking, and I thought of how my sister was always telling me that I needed to lighten up and have fun. That must be easy for her perfect self. Alas, maybe I did have a trait of the first-born type after all.

Truth be told, I was too serious, too much of a worrier. My mom said I got that from her.

Great!

I hoped I would outgrow it someday.

My mind started running away, and I had no reason to not follow it. This setting in the pub with these people playing games just didn't hold my interest. So, my mind landed in that strange, dark place that I don't traverse very often.

I can't surmise entirely how this place came to be inside my own head or heart, but it is real. And it has staying power. At times, I imagine that this place inside me came to be because I am a twin. An inadequate one at that. Sometimes, I've wondered if I'm just one small part of my sister that broke away from her being.

These thoughts are not about self-pity either—more like a realization. And furthermore, have nothing to do with my parents, who are perfect and amazing. They love Gini and me completely equally, so no one is to blame.

I have wondered sometimes if I'm supposed to be here. I've watched Gini be everything and do everything for so long that it has seemed she is the complete being, and maybe I am just the leftovers. Maybe she and I, combined, were meant to be one amazing creature, and something just went wrong—a biological hiccup.

It is only just a place—a place in my head. So, I have never taken it too seriously, even though it is seriously dark, and I've never told anyone about it either.

I haven't needed to be placed on suicide watch or anything like that. I'm sure that's what many people would assume: that I have had suicidal thoughts, but I haven't.

I remained in my dark mental space the rest of that night, and I noted that the walk back to the castle was still quiet. The quietness was surprisingly more eerie than when the wind was blowing and howling. Or screaming, as Joy would say.

Though I walked back to the castle with my cohort, I was miles away in my own mind.

CHAPTER TWELVE

EXCERPT FROM DIORVAL

One by one, they sat up in bed, their eyes glazed, still
asleep but moving with an eerie, unnatural precision.
It was as though invisible strings were pulling them
upright, their bodies rigid, faces blank. The man stood at
the center of the room, his presence thick in the air, and
with a slow, deliberate motion, he pointed to one of my
companions.

"What is your greatest fear?" His voice was firm as it
rippled through the room, commanding.

Without hesitation, the girl responded, her voice flat
and emotionless, as if the words were being drawn out
of her against her will. "Losing everything I love." The
answer was simple, terrifying in its honesty, and she
hadn't even opened her eyes.

I felt a cold chill crawl down my spine. I couldn't
believe what I was seeing. *This isn't real. It can't be.*
But I knew better. I wasn't dreaming. This was really
happening. I glanced around the room, my heart
pounding hard. Everyone was sitting up, their bodies stiff
like marionettes, their minds still trapped in sleep.

He moved on to the next one, his finger extending,
his gaze burning into them. Another question. Another
answer, as though they were helpless to resist the pull of
his influence. "What's your deepest regret?" he asked.

"I didn't tell him I loved him before he died," the girl beside me murmured.

I felt as if I'd gone mad, as though the fabric of reality was unraveling before my eyes. He was showing me his powers, bending the will of the others without even touching them. He had breached the boundary between worlds, manipulating those around me like a master puppeteer, even though he no longer truly belonged to this realm.

And I was the only one who saw it.

I stared at their faces, pale and lifeless, and knew that when they woke, they would have no memory of this. They would continue on, oblivious to what they had just been part of, and I was the only witness. The weight of that knowledge pressed down on me, making it hard to breathe.

What do you want from me? I thought, as if he could hear my silent question. But his attention never wavered from the others, as if my curiosity were part of his demonstration, part of his silent lesson.

The room seemed to pulse with a strange energy, the walls shifting ever so slightly, and I realized then that the only way anyone would ever know this had occurred would be if I told them. But I wouldn't. I couldn't.

I would never tell this to a living soul.

I could already feel the gravity of the secret sinking into my bones, a heavy, suffocating burden I would carry for the rest of my life. *I will take this experience to my grave. And even then*, I wondered, *will it truly be over?*

CHAPTER THIRTEEN

Kaya

Kaya clutched the flowers to her chest as she searched for the gravestone. Rain had just started with its cold onslaught, effectively dampening her hair and clothing, numbing her senses. Two rows beyond Luc's burial site, she found it. She could only stare at the name.

"Dear girl, I still don't believe it," Kaya whispered before bending to place the bouquet, the flowers growing heavy with the weight of raindrops.

Kaya jolted herself awake, crying out, "No! Claire!"

"It's OK, babe. Just a bad dream," Cole said, caressing Kaya's back as she sat up in bed, shaking.

"I couldn't find her." Kaya panted, out of breath. "We looked everywhere for her."

"It's just your anxiety playing tricks on you. Claire is OK. They would let us know if something were wrong."

"She's never been this far from home. She's alone," Kaya repeated for the hundredth time since her daughter left for the airport weeks ago.

"We have to let them grow up," Cole reminded.

"I know," Kaya said, massaging her temples before lying back.

"Thank God you don't worry about Gini as much, or you'd get no sleep at all."

"Claire is just more sensitive. She's just more—"

"Like you." Cole finished his wife's thought.

"Enough said, right?"

"Exactly."

Kaya rubbed her eyes and sighed.

"They are both going to be OK. Everything is going to be OK," Cole whispered.

She wanted to believe that more than anything.

CHAPTER FOURTEEN

Claire

Our bags rustled and clanged as we dumped the garbage we had collected for our art project. Prof. Stump's dump project, as Vic had named it. I had washed every piece of my refuse. I just wasn't sure if anyone else had, and I dreaded how this room was going to smell in the coming weeks. He moved across the front of the room in his customary strut, one eyebrow cocked in his ever-disgusted expression. He fingered the items piled on Joy's table as a bemused grin crossed his face.

Something about his disposition left me with a cold feeling inside. Something said that he enjoyed the grotesque nature of this project, and, more so, enjoyed the idea that this project may be revolting to his students. Sadist is the word that kept playing in my mind as I observed him.

His gaze swung quickly in my direction. I looked down, but not quickly enough.

"Mizz Boucher . . ."

My name hung in the air, freed from his cantankerous whine. The exaggerated way he said my name spoke unmistakably of his disdain for me.

I hesitantly looked up at him. He moved toward me the way a spider glides toward its prey, slowly at first as if it has all the time in the world and then swiftly, giving the death pounce. When he reached me, I may as well have been wrapped and bound in a web—there was no escaping.

I cringed at the cloud of halitosis that surrounded him as he spoke, "Did you not understand the assignment?"

He picked up one of my ginger ale cans and seared through my soul with his dead, black eyes.

I swallowed, feeling that rush of embarrassment crawl from my chest and up my neck to settle on my cheeks in its rouge-colored shame.

I blinked at him, my voice nowhere to be found.

His glare bore into me. "These are cans. They are recyclable, not garbage!" he snapped.

"I'm sorry," I stammered, lowering my eyes.

"Are you attempting to make a mockery of this assignment?" His voice boomed with his question.

I shuddered in the wake of his thunderous volume. I didn't dare look up at him, fearing I would be turned to stone instantaneously.

Barry and Vic entered the room just then, catching my eye. I mistakenly looked their way a nano-second too long.

"Mizz Boucher!" Professor Stump yelled again. "Can you hear me?"

I nodded, "Yes, Professor. I can hear you."

"Then tell the class what not to bring for this assignment!"

"Cans or any recyclables," I said weakly.

He leaned in, terrifyingly too close, and screamed, "What??"

"Don't bring cans or recyclables for this assignment," I managed to say coherently.

He powered up, puffing out his chest, seemingly ready to amp up another level, but Vic interrupted.

"We can't use cans?" Vic asked.

Stump snapped his head in Vic's direction with frightening predatory velocity.

Barry's eyes widened while Vic remained unfazed.

Some non-verbal exchange transpired between Vic and Stump. I imagined some law of the jungle code was at play—something along the lines of Vic could kick Stump's ass soundly if need be.

Stump suddenly straightened himself and slid his palms over the place above each ear as if slicking back his nonexistent hair. Then, he maneuvered his head, side to side and front to back, until his neck cracked.

Running his palms down his thighs, he answered, "No. You can't use cans."

Vic dropped his plastic bag in apparent exasperation, the sound of aluminum cans jostling and crashing. "I guess I have to start over."

"Me too," Barry said with a shrug.

"Me too," Joy said meekly, and others shared the same sentiment.

Stump grunted in annoyance, grumbling, "Unbelievable."

Vic flashed a charismatic smile and explained in the most disarmingly folksy way, "Professor, you see, we just don't have the same exposure to trash while we're here in Scotland. There's significantly less waste here. It's been quite a challenge finding items for this assignment. Not to mention,"—Vic chuckled—"this is a very disgusting endeavor. The last thing that crosses a person's mind when they have refuse is to hold on to it. It's counter-intuitive, ya know?"

Stump listened while stroking his oversized mustache with his right hand and holding his swollen belly with his left. I swear this man was a walking diet plan—my appetite always left whenever I laid eyes upon him.

"I don't mean any disrespect," Vic continued. "I hope you can understand our collective position and my need to play devil's advocate."

Stump huffed, and his posture relaxed as he relented. "Yeah, all right." He waved his hand impatiently and said, "Get out of here today. Go, collect more trash for tomorrow."

My complexion no longer burned with embarrassment, and my heart rate had returned to normal.

Everyone hastily packed up their bags. Absorbed in organizing my belongings, I lagged behind long enough for Stump to handily return to my table. His deadpan gaze held me hostage, his lips curling at the corner in mockery. "You got lucky this time," he said, his voice smooth, almost amused.

Joy called me from the doorway, "Claire, come on!"

Stump exhaled a sneer before strutting away. Grabbing my bag, I rushed out the door. I couldn't forget his words.

There he stood, his windswept hair perfectly smoothed. His shirt was taut against his chest and straining at times to remain intact over his muscular shoulders. I thought it might tear at the seams with each of his movements. He was a natural build.

Despite the obvious era differential between us, I was attracted to him in a way I'd never known before. OK, to be fair, I'd only dated one boy in high school so far. I was no connoisseur of the male species by any means.

He reached for my hand, his touch sending a ripple of warmth over my skin. As he pulled it gently to his lips, the world seemed to slow, his breath brushing softly against my knuckles. His eyes lingered on mine, deep and magnetic, as if they held a thousand secrets, inviting me to unravel them. For a long, unspoken moment, the air between us hummed with a promise—something just out of reach but undeniably present.

He tugged at my hand with a quiet urgency, pulling me closer until the space between us seemed to disappear. As I stepped toward him, he effortlessly twirled me, the world spinning around us in a dance only we knew. My breath caught as his voice, low and tender, wrapped around my name like a whispered secret, "Claire." The way he said it, like a soft plea or perhaps a promise, sent a shiver through me, leaving me breathless in his arms.

His gaze melted through me, igniting something deep within, unraveling every layer of my defenses. I waited, breath caught, heart pounding in the silence between us. His eyes held me captive, and I found myself clinging to the space between his next words, his next movement.

But just as I reached for the moment, I blinked—and he was gone.

The warmth of his presence faded like a half-forgotten dream, leaving only the ghost of his touch lingering in the air and the mystery of where he'd gone lingering in my soul.

But it was just a dream. And maybe he was just a ghost. The mystery of what had awakened me from my magical dream was solved as Julie walked through the bedroom door, likely from a visit to the bathroom. I glanced at my bedside clock. Only 3:17 a.m. The room held its usual chill to which I'd grown accustomed.

The wind outside howled in its familiar, eerie groan, and I wondered how I'd ever fall back asleep. My thoughts drifted, restless, to the dream I'd been pulled from—was it possible to return to it? I longed to see my handsome dream companion again, though the shadow of my unnerving professor lingered at the edges of my thoughts. Why had Stump appeared, his presence unsettling and out of place?

My mind wandered, trying to make sense of it, as if the dream held answers my waking life refused to give. Maybe my subconscious was compensating for something missing—a void I wasn't yet aware of. I clung to the notion, even though a deeper part of me sensed it might be more than just a harmless fantasy. Something in that dream felt unfinished, as if it were calling me back.

The kitchen was warm and inviting, filled with the comforting scent of freshly baked bread and herbs drying on the windowsill. I perched on a stool by the counter, watching as Effie kneaded dough with practiced ease, her fingers dusted with flour. The conversation had drifted to the castle's many legends, and Effie's tales fascinated me.

"Effie," I began, glancing toward the doorway as if expecting a ghost to drift by at any moment, "have you ever seen one of them? The spirits, I mean. You seem so certain they're here."

Effie smiled, her hands pausing in their rhythmic kneading. Her eyes took on a distant, almost dreamy look. "Aye, lass, I've had my fair share of encounters in this old place," she murmured. "And some experiences that are hard to forget."

My curiosity was piqued, my gaze fixed on Effie. "Tell me more. Have you ever seen Lady Red?"

Effie nodded slowly, her voice dropping to a near whisper. "Och, I have. Lady Red's as much a part of this castle as the stones in the walls. She's said to be the guardian of the laird's treasure, though what that treasure is, no one knows. Some say it's gold. Others say it is somethin' far more precious."

Effie's eyes took on a haunted look, her voice trembling slightly. "I saw her once, late one night when I'd stayed up tidying the dining hall. It was the wee hours when the night's as still as it ever gets, and there she was—standing by the fireplace, her face pale as the moon, her eyes filled with such sorrow, I could feel it, like a cold hand on my heart."

I shivered, captivated yet unsettled by Effie's description. "Did she say anything?"

Effie shook her head, pressing her lips together as if to lock in the memory. "Not a word. But she looked at me as if she were searchin' for somethin' or maybe someone. It felt as though she could see right through me, see things I didn't even know about myself. And then, just as quickly as she'd appeared, she was gone. A wisp of smoke in the shadows."

I leaned closer, hardly caring to breathe. "And what about the laird?"

Effie gave a slow nod, a glimmer of something reverent in her eyes. "The laird, aye. I've felt him too. He's a powerful presence, that one. I was just a girl the first time I knew he was there. It was a night like any other, and I was headin' down to the cellar to fetch more firewood. I'd always felt a strange energy down there, but this night, I felt somethin' different—a sense of someone watchin' me."

She paused, giving me a knowing look. "And then, I heard it—a low whisper, like the rustlin' of leaves, callin' me by name. I'd swear it was the laird himself, and though I never saw him, I could feel his presence as sure as I feel yours now."

A chill ran down my spine, though I felt an odd thrill, too, as if somehow closer to these spirits just by hearing about them. "What do you think he wanted?" I asked.

Effie shook her head, a touch of sadness in her eyes. "That, I canna say. But I think he's bound to this place for reasons only he understands. And Lady Red, well . . . she's tied to him, somehow. A kind of loyalty that goes beyond life and death. If ye're ever to meet them, lass," she added, patting my hand gently, "be sure to show respect. They've been here far longer than any of us, and this castle is as much theirs as it is ours."

I nodded, feeling a strange mixture of awe and warmth. "I think I've met one."

Effie's eyes twinkled. "That doesnae surprise me, lass. Ye've got a light about ye that would attract many a creature from this world and the next."

I swallowed, choosing my words carefully. "I feel something from him. It's like we're connected."

"Aye, the romance of the possibilities . . ." Effie's expression grew dreamy. "You have a connection, lass, or you wouldn't see him."

"It feels real," I confessed, sensing that Effie would honor my words, my feelings.

Effie gave me a kind smile, returning to her work. "It's a lovely feeling indeed, but keep yer feet firmly planted in this world. And remember, some things in life aren't meant to be explained, just meant to be experienced."

And Effie was right—I had never felt this way before.

CHAPTER FIFTEEN

Kaya

Kaya paused on the photo of Gini and Claire as toddlers. Gini used to love pushing Claire around in their doll stroller. A smile touched Kaya's lips, and a wistful warmth filled her. Cole strolled over to the sofa and touched his wife's shoulder, peeking to see the photo album.

"I'm glad you're old-fashioned like that, keeping photo albums." he said.

Kaya gave a backward glance at him, her face aglow with the memory of her girls. "Me too."

"Gini was so bossy." Cole chuckled.

"The CEO of the household."

"And CFO."

"Always saving her pennies."

"Stealing pennies too."

They laughed, and Cole came around, taking his place on the plush cushion. Kaya leaned toward him, his weight pushing the cushion deeper into the frame.

"I'm glad she outgrew that habit. Then there's Claire—so meek," Kaya said.

"But she could hold her own. Gini brought out her inner ninja a few times."

"True."

"She has to get fed up before she reacts."

"Also true."

Kaya and Cole spent the rest of the afternoon reminiscing about their daughters, their conversation weaving through the years like a well-loved story. The sweet scent of freshly squeezed lemonade mingled with the fragrance of the garden—their shared labor of love for almost two decades. As they strolled along the familiar paths, pulling a few weeds and picking flowers, they journeyed through their twins' many stories, each one evoking laughter and, at times, tears. Kaya hadn't realized just how much she needed this—this quiet moment of reflection, this gentle escape into memory.

But as the sun began its descent, casting long, golden shadows over the garden, a heaviness settled in Kaya's heart. Claire, especially, lingered on Kaya's mind with thoughts drifting like the soft breeze that whispered through the leaves. How bittersweet it was, the idea of letting them go. Soon, the girls would be adults—strong, capable, ready to embrace the world with all its trials and triumphs. Kaya knew this. She had always known. Yet something—something elusive—kept tugging at the edges of her peace. A shadow of a thought, a quiet, nagging worry about Claire that she couldn't quite shake.

As they neared the dinner hour, Kaya found herself breathing a little easier. She watched Cole with quiet adoration as he bent to pull another weed. How could she have ever imagined the life they'd built together? He had been a surprise—a beautiful, unexpected gift—showing up at her door when she had all but given up on love. Their life had been no fairy tale, but it had been beautiful in its own way. It had surpassed any dream she'd ever dared to dream. With Cole, she had become a mother, something she had never stopped longing for.

They decided on spaghetti for dinner, the simplicity of it comforting. But as they turned toward the house, Kaya's thoughts still lingered on Claire. There was something she wasn't seeing, something just out of reach, and it left her unsettled in the fading light.

CHAPTER SIXTEEN

EXCERPT FROM DIORVAL

His accent was so thick, and words rushed and frantic, that I struggled to understand the torrent of speech. But from the fragments I could piece together, I realized something chilling—he was trapped here. Not just in this place but between times, between dimensions, lost in a reality where the boundaries blurred and twisted. How it happened was a mystery, but one thing became horribly clear: he was on a mission, driven by a singular obsession—to save his wife from the lord of this cursed castle.

She had been taken, abducted like so many others, stolen for a sinister purpose. The lord needed her to bear more heirs because his own wife had become barren, her body unable to fulfill his insatiable desire for control. Diorval's voice trembled with barely restrained fury as he spoke of the lord's vile practices. This man—the lord—was no mere tyrant. He was a monster, preying on the surrounding villages, abducting young girls and women in the dead of night. Once taken, they vanished, their fates shrouded in silence and horror. Some were forced to serve as chambermaids, others as wet nurses. The youngest, strongest, were made into surrogate mothers, their wombs used to breed the next generation of heirs. None ever returned.

Diorval's village had been raided too many times to count, and the worst rumors followed each attack. Dark whispers of mutilation, madness, and worse. The fear in his eyes as he spoke told me that he had seen things—things he could barely bring himself to describe. But he was here now, driven to uncover the terrible truth. And more than that, to kill the lord and reclaim his wife before she was lost forever.

But as he spoke, his eyes changed, the intensity shifted and darkened. I shivered. His gaze settled on me with a strange, unnerving certainty. A cold realization washed over me. He thought I was her—his wife. In his madness, his desperation, he had mistaken me for the very woman he was trying to save. I was just an art student. Just Emily. The air between us grew thick, suffocating—his grip on reality faltering, while his grip on me tightened.

CHAPTER SEVENTEEN

Claire

H i, honey. I'm not trying to smother you, I promise," Mom said, her voice soft and affectionate. "I use so much restraint most of the time not to call you every day. Your dad said once a week is reasonable."

I smiled, hearing the warmth in my mother's voice. "Yes, Mom. Once a week is good."

"Oh, thank goodness! I couldn't go one more day without hearing from you. How are you? Is everyone treating my brilliant, genius girl kindly?" Mom's concern was wrapped in love, the kind that made my heart feel a little lighter.

I shifted the phone to my other ear, choosing my words carefully, "Yes, mostly. You know, people have their issues."

Mom cleared her throat, the familiar sound of her slipping into protector mode. "Just say the word, and I'll be on a plane."

I chuckled, comforted by my mom's fierce love. "No, Mom, it's OK. I know you would, but I got this. It's good for me—good practice for standing up for myself."

Mom paused. Her voice was gentle now. "Hmmm, OK. I trust you, sweetheart. But you know, you can always call. Your dad and I love hearing your voice."

I felt a swell of gratitude. "Thanks, Mom. I promise I'm OK. I love you. Tell Dad too."

"I will. We love you so much," Mom said, her voice brimming with sincerity and care.

"Bye, Mom."

"Goodbye, dear. Take care of yourself."

The call ended, and I felt the warmth of my mother's unwavering love, a comfort that stretched across the miles, wrapping around me.

As I climbed into bed that night—my heart peaceful—I heard his voice. "Sleep now, Claire" were the last words I heard.

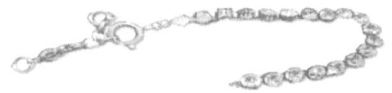

CHAPTER EIGHTEEN

Kaya

O h, doll-face. Come here. I can see your worry. Let Mommy
Grigio ease your troubles," Rita said, her brown eyes dancing
as she poured wine into a goblet as Kaya approached the table
at another favorite Italian restaurant of theirs, Dragzonetti's.

"Mommy Grigio," Kaya repeated, laughing.

"How are you holding up?"

"Shaky," Kaya answered, grabbing the glass and taking a healthy
swallow.

Rita chuckled. "Don't be shy. It's me. I've seen all your colors and
still love you and always will."

Kaya squeezed her best friend's hand. "I can't be shy with you. And
I feel like I already know the answer, but here goes: Am I nutty?"

"Duh."

"I mean, beyond my usual?"

Rita took a swallow of her red wine.

"Cole won't tell me if I've totally lost my mind."

"Um, he sleeps next to you. He wants to live, you know," Rita said
through a laugh.

"Yeah. I get it. I'm trying to give the girls enough space to grow and
become who they're meant to be. I just . . . never realized how terrifying
that would actually feel."

Rita gave her a knowing smile. "But don't forget the fears you've already stared down and conquered along the way. You got pregnant with twins later in life when motherhood wasn't even on your radar anymore. You've gotta give yourself more credit."

Kaya chuckled softly, appreciating her best friend's point. "You're right. I've had plenty of freak-out moments, but somehow, I always made it through. I kept my faith at every turn, and things just . . . worked out."

Rita's crisp white shirt practically glowed in the afternoon light, making her look like some wise angel with a bit of sass. Kaya couldn't help but smile as she continued, "For some reason, I'm not worried about Gini. It's Claire that keeps me up at night. Ever since she got to Scotland . . ."

Rita's brow furrowed, her concern deepening. "Is it Scotland itself, or just the fact she's so far away?"

"Both," Kaya admitted. "And add the fact that she's always had to deal with bullies. You know how she's quiet, kind, way too advanced for her age—maturity-wise and creatively. That makes her a target time and again."

Rita nodded thoughtfully. "I remember those issues with the bullies. But Claire's tough. She's grown some thick skin over the years. I'm sure by now she's learned how to handle those situations with some finesse."

Kaya sighed, staring down at her hands as though they held some hidden answers.

"Is there something else?" Rita's voice was gentle yet probing.

Kaya hesitated before confessing, "I've been having these . . . unsettling dreams. In every one of them, I'm searching for Claire, but no matter where I look, I can't find her."

Rita reached out, placing her warm hand over Kaya's. "That sounds like the nightmares all mothers have, especially when their kids are far away."

"Yeah." Kaya smiled, but only halfway. "It's just . . . I get this intense, foreboding feeling whenever I think about Claire. And it's worse since she's been in Scotland. I don't know what it is about that place, or maybe it's the castle she's staying in, but I feel like I need to warn her."

Rita's eyebrows began a slow, steady climb up her forehead as she stared at Kaya, her expression caught between confusion and mild alarm.

Kaya threw her hands up in frustration. "See what I mean? I sound insane! Warn her about what? I don't even know what I'm supposed to be warning her about!"

"Honey," Rita started softly, her voice apologetic, "I'm really sorry I joked earlier. I had no idea this was bothering you so much."

Kaya sighed, her shoulders slumping slightly. "I just don't know what to do with this feeling. It's like something's wrong, but I can't put my finger on it."

Rita thought for a moment, then gave a gentle nod. "You know, maybe you should call her more often. Check in."

Kaya's eyes brightened slightly, a flicker of hope returning. "You really think so?"

"Absolutely," Rita said with certainty. "If something's weighing on you this much, maybe a little extra contact will help put your mind at ease."

"You're right," Kaya agreed, her smile growing. "Maybe this nagging feeling will disappear if I do that."

Rita grinned. "And if not, well, you could always just show up at that creepy castle like the over-protective mom we all know you are."

Kaya laughed, rolling her eyes. "Oh, don't tempt me. You know I'm only one panicked thought away from booking a flight."

"Then Claire should definitely answer her phone more often," Rita teased, giving Kaya's hand a squeeze. "Just in case."

The two women laughed, but behind the humor, Kaya's worry lingered, a quiet storm waiting on the horizon.

CHAPTER NINETEEN

Claire

I closed my eyes. The present world melted away, and in its place emerged the vibrant hues and fragrant smells of my childhood. The memory unfurled in my mind like one of the roses in my mother's prized garden. I could hear the rustle of the wind moving through the rows of flowers, the buzz of the bees, and the soft, familiar hum of my mother's voice as she sang a tune I could never forget. It was a playful old melody about love measured in bushels and pecks, always ending with a warm squeeze around the neck.

We were eight, Gini and me, side by side as always, our small hands wrapped around the wooden handles of watering cans far too big for us. Gini had just finished watering the tulips and was now wiping dirt on her dress, grinning mischievously as Mother walked over.

"Gini, you know how to make a fun mess in the garden," Mother chided, though her soft smile belied any seriousness.

Gini, always the cheeky one, shrugged. "Flowers like a little mess. It makes them grow better. Right, Claire?"

I laughed. My own hands were covered in soil as I gingerly patted down the earth around the daisies. "Maybe that's why you've always grown faster than me. More mess."

Father's chuckle rumbled from the other side of the garden, where he was pruning a patch of roses. "They're not wrong, you know," he called. "Sometimes a bit of chaos helps things bloom even brighter."

We giggled as we ran over to him, our shoes crunching on the gravel path. We always loved helping our father with the roses, his pride and joy. He bent down, handing Gini a pair of gardening shears, showing her how to snip the deadheads gently. "See, just like this. You don't want to hurt the stem."

"Like this?" Gini asked, carefully mimicking his motion.

"Perfect," our father said with a wink. "You've got a natural touch."

I stood nearby, entranced by the rich smell of the roses. "Why do the roses always smell so different from the other flowers?" I asked, my small voice soft in the warmth of the summer air.

Mother, now kneeling beside us, smiled as she placed her hand on my shoulder. "Roses have been through more, darling. They have to be strong to grow their thorns. The struggle makes their beauty even more special. Your dad told me that years ago."

My parents exchanged a look of deep connection and understanding that only the two of them were privy to.

I nodded, reaching out to touch one of the delicate blooms. Gini, always brimming with energy, plucked a petal and placed it on my nose, laughing when it stuck. "You've got a rose for a nose!"

We laughed until we fell to the ground, rolling among the lavender and marigolds, our joy as radiant as the blooms around us. Mother joined in, lying on the grass with her arms outstretched, eyes closed as if to soak up the essence of the day.

"I wish we could stay here forever," I whispered, my heart full of the peace that only the garden could bring.

Father's voice came from behind us, soft and steady, "We can't stay here forever, little one, but the garden will always be here, waiting. And as long as you carry these moments with you, they'll never leave you."

I felt the truth of those words, even now, as I sat in silence, years away from that day. If I concentrated hard enough, I could remember that deep fragrance of the roses even over the musty smell of the castle. Gini's laughter echoed in my ears, as if we were still lying side by side among the flowers.

In the memory, Gini leaned over, her face close to mine as she whispered, "You know, we'll have our garden someday. Bigger than this one. With every flower in the world! And we'll never let anyone pick the roses."

My heart ached with the sweetness of it. I had forgotten about that promise. But in this moment, I could almost believe in that dream again, as if we were still those two little girls in the sun, dreaming of a world where everything bloomed forever.

"Do you think we'll still be doing this when we're old?" I had asked, my voice barely more than a breath.

Gini had squeezed my hand. "Of course. We'll be old, wrinkly, and still planting flowers. Together. I promise."

In the quiet of the present, a single tear slipped down my face. The garden had been more than a place. It was a promise of the unbreakable bond Gini and I shared. I wiped the tear away and smiled softly, my heart filled with the warmth of that long-ago summer. And then I carefully sealed it away in my heart.

CHAPTER TWENTY

Claire

The soft afternoon light filtered through the castle windows and into the art studio, where Ms. Haas taught her calm, lovely, and wonderful painting class. I thanked heavens for a professor so different than Stump. Stump the Grump is what my cohort was quietly calling him. More like Stump the Maniac if you asked me, but that didn't rhyme.

Ms. Haas had given us our instructions and went to the front corner to do some painting herself. It seemed my cohort felt the same relief I did in having this stable, normal presence from an instructor. Even though we were not expected to work quietly, no one chatted. All eight of us got absorbed in our respective paints and canvases.

With the easels scattered around the room and the familiar scent of fresh paint filling the air, the studio felt like a sanctuary. I dipped my brush into a vibrant shade of blue, my mind lost in the gentle rhythm of my strokes. Across from me, Joy was equally focused, her canvas coming to life with swirling shades of orange and gold.

After a few quiet moments, Joy broke the silence, her voice warm and thoughtful. "You know, I've never met anyone who loves painting as much as I do."

I smiled, glancing up from my canvas. "Same here. It's not exactly something most people talk about, right?"

Joy laughed softly. "No, not really. Everyone's always talking about what's practical or productive. But painting? That's something else."

I nodded, pausing my brush mid-stroke. "It's like a world of its own. Every time I paint, it feels like time slows down and nothing else matters."

Joy and I had a quiet understanding between us, as if we had both been waiting to find someone who saw painting the way we did.

Joy set her brush down, leaning back slightly. "How did you start? Painting, I mean."

My thoughts drifted back to a sunny summer morning. "I think I was five years old. I remember one early summer morning when I caught my dad sneaking out the kitchen door with his paintbrushes in hand. That was the day I discovered his early morning ritual: painting in the flower garden. I followed him and asked if I could paint too."

I paused and, with a sigh, continued my recollection. "He taught me the basics, and he showed me what it was to love and feel passionate about a hobby. I think after that day, he got up even earlier so that he could have his time alone painting before I joined him, but he never denied me. And I also think that detail made me love painting all the more.

My dad was so talented that I felt like I could never get to his level. The splendor he could ransom from a flower always boggled my mind. And there I was, painting flowers, the trees, and the sky."

I found myself smiling as I recalled those mornings, the sunlight warm on my skin and the quiet hum of nature all around me. "Painting always felt like a way to hold on to moments with my dad, like I was capturing pieces of us in my own little way."

Joy's face lit up. "That's beautiful, Claire. Your dad sounds amazing."

"He was," I said. "Still is. What about you? How did you start out?"

Joy's expression turned wistful as she twirled a brush between her fingers. "My grandma, actually. She was an artist. Not professionally or anything, but she used to paint these huge landscapes in her living room. I remember when I was around seven, she'd let me sit beside her while she worked, and she'd give me a little canvas of my own. I remember the first time I painted a sunset with her—well, it was supposed to be a sunset, but it mostly looked like a bunch of colors splattered everywhere."

Joy and I laughed together, the image of a tiny Joy trying to capture the complexity of a sunset in her childish, innocent way—and likely messy way.

"She never cared about the mess, though," Joy continued, her voice softening. "She'd always look at whatever I painted and say, 'You've got the heart of an artist, Joy. It's not about getting it to someone's standard of right. It's about feeling it.' And that's what stuck with me. It wasn't about making something perfect—it was about letting what's inside you come out on the canvas."

I leaned in slightly, captivated by her story. "That's so wonderful. Your grandma sounds like the kind of person who really understood what art is about."

Joy nodded, her eyes bright with fondness. "She really did. Even now, whenever I paint, I feel like she's still sitting beside me, encouraging me to just . . . let go."

For a moment, we just sat in silence, both absorbed in the warmth of our memories, the love we had received from the family who introduced us to painting. It felt like a rare and precious connection, the kind that went beyond just shared interests. It was as if our love for painting had been nurtured in the same garden of creativity and care, even though our paths had been different.

I smiled, feeling a deep sense of gratitude and understanding. "Yeah. It's like we're carrying the love with us every time we pick up a brush."

We both turned back to our canvases, and the room filled with a comfortable silence. But now, the space between us felt that much lighter, more open, as if we had shared not just our stories but a piece of our hearts.

As I dipped my brush into a new color, I glanced at Joy and said, "You know, we should paint together more often."

Joy's smile widened, and she winked as she said, "Good thing we're table buddies in this class."

"Oh, yeah. That and maybe outside of class too," I added.

"For sure," she agreed.

I looked forward to some weekend painting sessions with my friend, which I was sure would help the loneliness of the weekend pass more quickly and hopefully ease the eerie feeling that sometimes overwhelmed me when I was in the art studio alone. Also, I looked forward to more talks with her. I could sense that she was just as lonely as I was.

I was finishing up the final touches on my painting when Barry burst into the studio, as he always did—full of energy, like a gust of wind had blown him in. He had a habit of moving quickly, his curly hair bouncing as he approached, eyes wide with excitement.

"Claire! There she is, the Van Gogh of our time," Barry announced dramatically, waving his arms in mock reverence.

I smirked, dipping my brush into a bright yellow. "Oh, please. If I'm Van Gogh, then you're Picasso—chaotic but somehow pulling it off."

Barry let out a loud, exaggerated gasp, placing his hand over his heart. "I accept that as a high compliment! But seriously, have you looked at your work? You've got something, Claire. I don't know what it is, but it's like your paintings feel alive, you know?"

I felt myself blush a little but kept my eyes on the canvas. "Thanks, Barry. You're just saying that because you want me to help you with your project later."

"Well, yes, but also, no! I mean it!" Barry pulled up a stool beside me, his voice dropping to a more sincere tone. "You've got that kind of natural talent that people dream about. Do you even realize how rare that is?"

I shrugged, feeling a little shy under the weight of his praise. "I guess I've just always been around art. My dad paints too, so I grew up watching him."

Barry's eyes lit up. "Oh, right! I keep forgetting your dad is this big local artist back home. What is that like? Having a dad who actually, you know, sells his art? That's huge! Not everyone can make it like that."

I smiled, thinking of Dad's cozy studio back in our small town, the walls lined with canvases depicting his famous pretentious frogs, still-life flowers, and scenes from Gini's and my childhood, mostly in the garden. "Yeah, it's pretty cool. He sells his paintings mostly to people in town and tourists, I suppose. He's really well-known there."

"Man, that's amazing," Barry said, his voice filled with admiration. "It's one thing to be a good artist, but to be able to sell your work locally and have people actually want to buy it? That's, like, the dream, isn't it? Does he have his own gallery or something?"

"Not exactly. It's pretty cool the local restaurants and cafes feature his work. He's got a loyal following there—people know him for capturing the local beauty, you know? You know the tourist traffic is pretty regular too. And he paints fast. I think he cranks out three or four pieces a week sometimes," I explained, chuckling.

Barry whistled, "That's wild. Does he ever give you advice, like, 'Claire, use more blue!' or 'Why don't you paint something less ab-stract?'"

I laughed, nodding my head. "Oh, all the time! He's got opinions about everything. Sometimes, he'll walk in while I'm working and say something like, 'Hmm, that shade's not quite right.' or 'You could add more contrast there.' It drives me crazy, but he's always right."

Barry threw his head back, laughing. "Of course he is! He's a pro! Does he ever, like, sell your stuff too? You could be the next big thing in your town."

"Not yet," I said with a grin. "But who knows? Maybe I'll slip one of my paintings in with his next batch and see if anyone notices."

"Oh, that would be brilliant! And then, when it sells, you can be like, 'See, Dad? I've got skills too!'" Barry leaned in, his voice taking a conspiratorial tone. "But, seriously, you should think about it. If people in your town already love his work, they'd probably go crazy for yours."

I felt my eyebrows shoot upward. "You think so?"

"Are you kidding? You've got that same magic, Claire. It's like you see the world differently, and you know how to put that feeling on canvas. People would eat it up."

I smiled, feeling the warmth of his words settle in my chest. "Thanks, Barry. That means a lot."

Barry grinned and gave me a playful nudge. "Don't mention it. But when you're famous and people are lining up for paintings, just remember who gave you the idea first, OK? A little credit wouldn't hurt."

I laughed, giving him a light shove in return. "You've got a deal. I'll put your name on the back of my first sold painting."

"Perfect! That's all I ask," Barry said with a wink. He stood up, looking over my shoulder at the painting I was working on. "Now, what do you say we both become famous by tackling this next assignment? Or, at least, you help me not completely ruin mine?"

I rolled my eyes, shaking my head, feeling amused. "Alright, Picasso. Let's see what you've got."

⁊✿⁊

The art studio was bathed in a silvery glow as I sat at my easel. I recognized that this was another dream by the vibrant tapestries hanging over the stony walls. He was there in the shadows, watching as my brush glided over the canvas.

"Claire, I could watch ye paint for hours. The way ye see the world captures my imagination and my heart, lass," he said in a voice laced with admiration.

A tingle ran through me as his words touched my heart. "Thank you," was all I could manage as shyness bubbled up within me.

His persistence unraveled me on a level I'd never known before. I fought to not be consumed by thoughts of him in my waking hours, but at night … at night, I couldn't wait to see his face and hear his voice.

"I'd do anything to spend time with ye, Claire. Do ye know that, lass?" he asked.

I stopped mid-stroke, the brush resting against the canvas. "But that's impossible," I said. "Isn't it?"

"Lass, love can work miracles—you wouldn't be here otherwise,' he explained softly.

My heart swelled as the conviction of his words settled into me

"Ye're worth finding." His words faded as the dream blurred into darkness.

I lay in bed, replaying his words and letting their warmth lull me back to sleep.

CHAPTER TWENTY-ONE

Kaya

The sunny day spilled through the tall bay windows of Kaya's Victorian home, dappling light onto the wood floors as the lace curtains fluttered gently in the warm summer breeze. Kaya sat at the coffee table in the parlor, her fingers tracing the rim of her teacup. She stared out toward the quiet, tree-lined street, but her mind was miles away—across the ocean, in fact—hovering over Scotland.

Ivy sat across from her, sipping tea as if the weight of the world weren't sitting squarely on Kaya's shoulders. With her bright eyes and silver hair pulled into a loose bun, Ivy always seemed more youthful than her years. She noticed the distant look in her daughter's eyes and sighed that dramatic way only Ivy could.

"All right, spill it. What's gnawing on you, sweetheart? I haven't seen you look this serious since you found out you needed to hire a gardener or be fined by the beautification committee almost twenty years ago." Ivy winked. "We all know how that turned out."

Kaya looked up, managing a small smile. "I'm just thinking about Claire, you know. Scotland feels so far away, and it's her first time really being on her own."

Ivy leaned back in her chair, a twinkle in her eye. "Ah, yes, the age-old worry: What if my brilliant, capable, beautiful daughter, who's been dreaming of studying art since she could hold a crayon, somehow forgets everything I ever taught her and falls apart without me?"

Kaya couldn't help but laugh at her mother's exaggeration, though the knot in her chest remained. "I know, I know. She's grown up, and she's strong. But I can't help it, Mom. She's so far away, and what if—"

"What if she meets a wild Highlander and runs off to live in a castle surrounded by sheep?" Ivy interrupted, her voice filled with mock horror. "And you'll be stuck flying to Scotland for family holidays, trying to learn Gaelic and herding cattle? The horror, Kaya! The horror!"

Kaya rolled her eyes, but the tension in her shoulders eased. "I'm serious, Mom."

"So am I! You should start brushing up on your sheep-herding skills. Or maybe take up bagpipes. We've got to be prepared for the worst."

Ivy grinned wickedly, but after a beat, her expression softened. "Sweetheart, I know how much you worry. It's part of the job description. But Claire's got your spirit. She's out there, painting her heart out, chasing her dreams, and probably charming the socks off everyone she meets."

Kaya nodded, biting her lip. "I just miss her. I want to be there for her if things get hard."

"Of course, you do," Ivy said, her voice gentler now. "But part of this whole parenting thing is learning to let them go. You did your job, Kaya. You raised her with love and courage and all the tools she needs. Now it's her turn to figure out how to use them. And don't forget, she's got your stubbornness too. You're both like old oaks—you don't bend easily."

Kaya sighed, feeling the familiar mix of love and helplessness. "I guess I just wish I knew for sure that she's happy. That she's OK."

Ivy leaned back in her chair again, crossing her arms. "Let me ask you something. When you were Claire's age, setting out into the world, did you tell me every time something went wrong? Did you call me the minute you had a rough day?"

Kaya smiled ruefully. "No, but I knew you were there if I needed you."

"And Claire knows the same," Ivy said, nodding firmly. "She knows you're just a phone call away, and she'll reach out when she needs to. Until then, you've got to trust that she's out there, living her life, just like you did."

Kaya's smile grew, a bit of the weight lifting from her heart. "You always make things sound so simple."

Ivy waved a hand dismissively. "That's because I'm a genius, darling. Or at least, I'm very good at pretending to be one."

They both laughed, the sound light and easy, as the summer breeze continued to stir the air around them. For a moment, Kaya felt the tension melt away, soothed by her mother's wisdom and her irreverent humor.

Ivy set her teacup down with a clatter. "Now, enough of this brooding. Let's do something productive. We could pick some flowers from the garden and make a bouquet with Claire in mind, or—better yet—go shopping and have martinis."

Kaya's eyes lit up at the suggestion of time in the garden, even though she knew her mother preferred the latter. "I'd love to make a bouquet dedicated to Claire."

Ivy winked. "There you go! And who knows? Maybe while we're out there, you'll get a call from Scotland telling you all about her latest masterpiece. Or at least about how she managed to survive without you for another week."

Kaya laughed, standing up and pulling her mother into a warm hug. "Thanks, Mom. For everything."

Ivy patted her back, her voice full of affection and just the right amount of mischief. "Always, darling. Now, come on, let's go pick those flowers and mix a martini. If Claire does fall in love with a Highlander, we'll need to plan a wedding. I'm so ready for that."

Kaya smiled at her mother, wanting to share in the moment of optimism despite her turbulent heart.

CHAPTER TWENTY-TWO

Claire

The studio buzzed with the friendly chatter of my cohort that afternoon, accompanied by the steady hum of brushes against canvas. I focused on my work, blocking out everything except the vibrant swirl of colors in front of me. I loved these moments—the way the rest of the world seemed to disappear when I painted. But today, that peace was shattered by someone approaching, heels clicking sharply against the studio floor.

Julie.

I felt a tightness in my chest before I even saw her. Julie had been hovering ever since we arrived in Scotland. I guess she was just not getting over the fact that I was accepted into the art program as a high school student. And she hadn't made her unhappiness about it a secret.

"Well, well, well." Julie's voice dripped with sarcasm as she stopped beside my easel. "If it isn't our little prodigy. You know, Claire, some of us had to actually finish high school before getting into this class."

I kept my eyes on my canvas, refusing to let Julie's words get to me. "I'm just here to learn, Julie. Same as everyone else."

Julie let out a short, mocking laugh as she flipped her long, wavy blonde hair back with the flick of her wrist. "Oh, please. You're not like everyone else, and you know it. You're the *exception*, right? The special little high schooler who gets to skip ahead. Must be nice."

My brush paused for a second, but I didn't respond. I wasn't going to give Julie the satisfaction of a reaction.

Julie stepped closer, her voice dropping to a low, venomous whisper, "You think you're so much better than the rest of us, don't you? Just because you're a 'natural talent' or whatever garbage they say about you. But you don't deserve to be here."

The words hit harder than I was ready to absorb, but I forced myself to stay calm. I'd heard the whispers from other students, the gossip about how it wasn't fair that I'd been allowed into the program early. But hearing it from Julie with the sharp edge of bitterness made it sting.

"I don't think I'm better than anyone," I said quietly, my grip tightening on my brush. "I'm just trying to do my best."

Julie snorted, crossing her arms. "Your best? Sure. But don't think for a second that everyone's impressed. Some of us have worked years to get into this class, and then you just waltz in like you belong here. Like you've earned it."

I looked up, meeting Julie's cold gaze. "I worked hard too. Just because I'm younger doesn't mean I haven't earned my place."

Julie's lips twisted into a cruel smile. "Hard work, huh? Or maybe it's just because your daddy's some small-town artist who thinks he can buy you a free pass into the world. Is that it, Claire? Riding on Daddy's coattails?"

My heart pounded hard in my chest. I could feel the heat rising in my face, my hands trembling slightly. That was low, even for Julie. My father had nothing to do with my being here—I'd earned it on my own. But Julie's words cut deep.

"That's not true," I said, my voice steady despite the tightness in my throat. "I'm here because of my work, not because of my dad."

Julie's eyes narrowed, probably sensing that she'd hit a nerve. "Oh, sure. Keep telling yourself that. But deep down, you know you don't belong here. You're just a little girl playing in the big leagues, and eventually, everyone's going to see that. Stump sees it. Big-time!"

I clenched my jaw, trying to keep my composure. I didn't understand why Julie had such a grudge against me, but it was clear that jealousy fueled her cruelty. The sad part was I had admired Julie's talent when I first saw her artwork. But now, all I could see was someone desperate to tear me down.

"I don't know why you hate me so much, Julie," I said, standing up and facing her. "But your jealousy doesn't change the fact that I worked hard to be here. And I'm not going anywhere."

Julie's smile faltered, her eyes flashing with anger. "You're so full of yourself, Claire. But trust me, your time will come. You'll slip up, and when you do, I'll be right there to remind everyone that you never really belonged."

With that, Julie turned on her heel and walked away, her words lingering like poison in the air.

I stood there for a moment, my heart still racing. I took a deep breath, trying to shake off the tension that clung to me like a shadow. I knew Julie was wrong—I had earned my place here. But even so, the weight of Julie's bitterness hung heavy on me, leaving me feeling more alone than ever, even in a room full of people.

Still, I wasn't going to let Julie get to me. Not today. Not ever.

I sat back down, picked up my brush, and let the colors on my canvas flow, determined to prove that I deserved to be here—no matter what anyone said.

Joy came over with a curious look in her eyes and asked, "Did Julie give you some compliments on your beautiful work?"

I could tell Joy sincerely wished that that had been my conversation with Julie. I wasn't going to reveal what really had been said. "Yeah, something like that. She thinks I have a great eye for color."

"You really do, Claire," Joy agreed with a smile.

I tried so hard not to believe Julie's cruel words, not let them seep in.

CHAPTER TWENTY-THREE

Claire

The night was still, the air thick with the sweet scent of heather from the Scottish countryside outside my window. I had been dreaming of him again—the mysterious boy I couldn't quite place but felt inexplicably drawn to. For weeks, the dreams had been coming, vivid and haunting, leaving me breathless when I awoke. I always saw his eyes first, deep and stormy like the Scottish skies, watching me from the mists of time.

Tonight felt different, though. As I lay in my bed, the line between sleep and waking blurred, and I sensed his familiar presence lingering in my room, stronger than ever before. A chill ran down my spine, but it wasn't fear—something else thrummed beneath the surface.

Suddenly, the soft sound of footsteps broke the stillness of the room, and my heart leaped in my chest. I sat up slowly, my breath catching as I looked toward the shadowy corner.

He stepped into the light.

Tall and broad-shouldered, with wavy black hair, the boy before me was handsome as ever. His features were sharp and noble. His eyes, a piercing shade of gray, locked onto mine, filled with an ancient knowing. He wore a Highlander's garb from centuries past, a dark green plaid draped across his strong form, and a faint smile, both charming and mysterious, played on his lips.

My breath caught as I stared at him, my mind racing to make sense of what was happening. "You're real," I whispered, my voice barely more than a breath.

The boy—Angus, I realized instinctively—stepped closer, his movements graceful, otherworldly. His voice was rich with the lilt of a long-lost Scottish dialect. "Aye, lass. I'm real enough."

His smile deepened, full of warmth and something else—something like admiration.

I swallowed, my heart pounding in my chest. "I've been dreaming about you for weeks. Who are you?"

"Angus MacLean," he said, bowing his head slightly, a touch of old-world chivalry in his gesture. "I hail from the thirteenth century—though it seems time no longer holds me as it once did."

My head spun. A ghost. I had known it, deep down, but hearing it made everything feel so much more surreal. "Why . . . why me? Why have you been haunting my dreams?"

Angus chuckled softly, the sound like velvet. "Haunting ye? I wouldn't call it that, lass. I've been drawn to ye. Since the moment I first saw ye. I knew I had to reach ye. Yer spirit . . . it called to mine." His eyes softened, and he stepped even closer, his presence almost tangible now. "Ye've awakened something in me that's been asleep for centuries."

My heart raced as he spoke. His words, his voice, the way he looked at me—it was as if we were connected by something deeper than time itself. "I don't understand. Why me? What am I to you?"

Angus reached out, and though I knew he was not of this world. His hand brushed mine, sending a shiver through me. "Ye're everything," he whispered, his gaze locked on mine. "In life, I fought for my clan, for honor, for land—but I never knew love."

His words made my heart flutter. "You don't even know me," I whispered, though part of me felt like he did—like we had always known each other, somehow.

Angus's eyes darkened with emotion, his expression softening as he held my gaze. "Nay, lass. I do know ye. I've known ye from the moment our souls touched. Ye've haunted me as much as I've haunted ye. In my dreams, I saw yer face, yer strength, yer light. Ye see the world beautifully. Like I've told you before, I see that in yer paintings. And now, now I canna stay away."

My breath hitched as he moved closer still, his presence almost overwhelming yet comforting at the same time. His words were like a spell, weaving around me, pulling me in. I could feel something magical between us.

"I've waited lifetimes for ye," Angus murmured, his voice barely above a whisper now.

He was so close I could see the flicker of something ancient in his eyes—an intensity that made me feel as if I were standing at the edge of a vast, untouchable history. "And I'll wait as long as it takes, Claire."

I trembled, my heart pounding harder still, my mind spinning with the impossible reality of it all. But despite the strangeness of it, despite the centuries that separated us, something deep inside me knew—this was real. This was him.

"I don't even know what to say," I whispered, my voice shaky yet sure.

Angus's smile softened, his hand hovering just above mine again as if testing the limits of the space between us. "Ye dinnae have to say anything, lass. Just know that I'm here, and I'll no' leave ye. I am compelled to protect ye when I can. Ye deserve that much."

And in that moment, I knew the truth of his words. I felt it in the way he looked at me, in the way his presence filled the room with warmth and a sense of belonging I hadn't realized I was missing. Whatever this was, whatever bond had tied me to Angus across time and space, it was undeniable.

With his whisper-light touch, he spun me around, smiling unabashedly at me. His warm eyes danced, and he did a little jig and bowed at me.

I giggled at his display of cuteness and charm, the depths of both so endearing to me.

I got the sense that this was only just the beginning with Angus.

I jolted awake, my breath coming in shallow gasps as my eyes flew open, the remnants of the dream clinging to me like a mist. The room was filled with the sounds of my sleeping cohort. The faint chirping of crickets outside my window drifted in whenever the rhythm of the wind slowed. For a moment, I lay there, my heart racing.

Angus.

His name echoed in my mind, as real as the warmth of his gaze and the soft, lilting sound of his voice. I could still feel him—the way his presence had wrapped around me, strong and steady, filling the space between us with something electric. But as I blinked in the darkness, reality slowly settled back in, and the vividness of the dream slipped through my fingers like sand.

I sat up in bed, pushing my hair back from my damp forehead. My heart hadn't slowed to its normal pace yet as a mixture of exhilaration and disappointment swirled inside me. It had felt so real—so incredibly, achingly real. The intensity of his words, his gaze, the way he had made me feel as though we had been destined to find each other—it all lingered in my chest, making it hard to breathe.

But he was gone. Just a dream.

My fingers tightened around the sheets, frustration bubbling up. I wanted to hold on to the connection I'd felt in my dream, but with every passing second, it became harder to grasp. It was like trying to catch the wind.

I closed my eyes, letting out a long breath, willing myself to relax. But the truth gnawed at me. Angus wasn't real. He was just a figment of my imagination, something my mind had conjured in the stillness of the night. And yet, the dream had left me trembling, my heart racing and fluttering with an unfamiliar awakening.

How could something that wasn't real feel like this?

I sighed, my hands trembling as I hugged my knees to my chest. The dream had been so vivid, his voice still ringing in my ears, full of that deep, resonant warmth. He had felt so close, as if I could just reach out and touch him—and for a moment, I swore I had. I could still feel the ghostly warmth of his hand hovering above mine, the way his eyes had looked into mine.

My heart twisted at the memory. I had wanted it to be real—so badly.

But it was only a dream.

I swallowed the lump in my throat and glanced out the window. The moon hung low in the sky, only a sliver. My mind swirled with thoughts of Angus—his piercing gray eyes, his rugged handsomeness, the way his voice had said my name like it meant something more than just a word.

I felt a strange sense of loss, as though I'd just been pulled away from something, or someone, I wasn't ready to let go of. My hands brushed the soft fabric of my blanket, and for a moment, I wished I could slip back into sleep, into the dream, where he was waiting for me—where it all made sense, where the impossible seemed possible.

But no matter how hard I tried, reality was settling in like the cold light of dawn.

I exhaled, a mixture of exhilaration and disappointment tugging at me. Despite the ache in my chest, a small part of me felt alive in a way I hadn't before. Dream or not, Angus had awakened something inside me—a spark I hadn't known was there, a feeling that I couldn't quite put into words.

Maybe it had only been a dream. But in that dream, for just a little while, I had felt something real.

And deep down, I couldn't shake the feeling that this wasn't the last I'd see of Angus. Dream or not, I felt drawn to him—as though our story was just beginning.

With a small, wistful smile, I lay back down, closing my eyes and letting the memory of his presence linger a little longer. My excitement was building more each day.

CHAPTER TWENTY-FOUR

EXCERPT FROM DIORVAL

The room was eerily still tonight, the moonlight seeping through the curtains. While I lay in bed, my mind whirled with a strange unease I couldn't quite place. Everything seemed normal, yet something felt off. The shadows in the corners of the room shifted subtly, as though the walls themselves were exhaling, stretching. I blinked, my heart giving a quick, uneasy flutter.

I turned over, pulling the blanket closer around me, hoping to drift back into sleep. But as my eyes scanned the room again, the hairs on the back of my neck prickled. The door. I didn't understand what I was seeing. The door had been on the left side of the room since the day I'd arrived here but now—now it was on the right.

I sat up, staring at the door. My pulse quickened. Was I dreaming before, or was I dreaming now? I rubbed my eyes and glanced around the room again, my gaze settling on the wardrobe at the far end. Only . . . the wardrobe wasn't where it had been either. It had moved, shifted somehow, closer now, as though it had crept forward when I wasn't looking.

I couldn't breathe for a moment, panic beginning to tighten its grip on my chest. I swung my legs over the side of the bed, my bare feet hitting the floor, cold and solid. *It's just a dream*, I told myself. *I'm still asleep.* But my surroundings felt too vivid, too real—the cool air brushing my skin, the faint creaks of the wood floor settling. This wasn't a dream. This was something else.

I stood, my legs trembling as I walked toward the window, hoping for some sense of normalcy. But as I approached, the room seemed to ripple around me, the walls bending in on themselves in ways that made my stomach turn. The floor shifted beneath my feet, elongating, twisting, as if the entire space were being reshaped by an invisible hand.

A low hum filled the room, barely audible. My heart thumped as I nervously looked around. It wasn't the same anymore. The ceiling had risen impossibly high, vanishing into a dark void above me. The walls stretched, warping and bending in directions that defied logic, the furniture contorting into strange, impossible shapes. The door—the only exit—was now nowhere in sight.

"What's happening?" I whispered. I put my hand on my chest as though I could steady my own pounding heart. The room was closing in on me and yet expanding at the same time. I wasn't sure which way was up, my sense of space and time unraveling before my eyes.

And then I saw him. Diorval.

He materialized out of the shadows, his figure tall and cloaked in something darker than the night. His eyes gleamed, as though they held secrets of worlds beyond my comprehension. He stepped forward, his presence both commanding and otherworldly, blurring the line between dream and nightmare.

"You feel it, don't you?" Diorval's voice was a whisper that echoed unnaturally in the warping room. "The veil between worlds. It's thinner than you think."

My legs trembled so violently, I thought I might collapse. "What . . . what is this?" I heard my own voice, shaky and weak, asking, "Am I dreaming?"

Diorval smiled. "You're not dreaming," he said softly. "You're seeing what you could never see before—the world beyond this one. I have the power to open it for you."

My chest constricted. "No, I don't want to see any more. Please make it the way it normally is."

But the room still changed, melting from the familiar into something unrecognizable. The floor beneath my feet rippled like water, and I stumbled, feeling as though I were sinking into the very ground. The walls twisted again, bending at impossible angles, stretching into a labyrinth that seemed infinite. I couldn't breathe, couldn't think—everything felt like it was spiraling out of control.

"You can't run from it," Diorval murmured calmly despite the chaos around us. "This is what lies beyond your world. This is the truth. I can take you there."

"No!" I yelled as I scrambled backward, my back hitting a wall that hadn't been there moments before. I clawed at it, trying to find something solid, something real to anchor myself, but everything was shifting—turning into something unfamiliar.

I looked at Diorval, pleading, "Please . . . stop this."

He exhaled slowly and then raised his hand. The room rippled again, but this time, the pulsing slowed and the walls steadied. The unbearable sensation of being trapped between worlds began to fade, the warped dimensions retreating until the room resembled the way I had known it.

I slumped against the wall, my body shaking, breaths ragged as I stared at Diorval. He stepped closer, and I could see compassion brimming in his eyes.

"I just wanted to show you," he said softly. "I didn't mean to scare you. I just wanted you to understand so you know what to expect if you decide to come back to me, my love."

I couldn't speak. I had no words to respond at the moment. My mind still reeled from the terror of the experience. As Diorval's presence began to fade into the shadows once more, I was left standing in the eerily quiet room. My heart still pounded in my ears.

As the last traces of his energy dissipated, I realized that this wasn't the last time I'd feel the world shift.

CHAPTER TWENTY-FIVE

Claire

I was dreaming again. This time, I sat in my childhood bedroom. The soft glow of moonlight streamed through the window, casting ethereal shadows across the room. My eyes wandered to the canvas paintings I had completed over the years, each a delicate floral testament to my deepest passions. These flowers, vibrant and alive under my brush, had always been my sanctuary, my silent confidantes in a world that often seemed too loud.

Amid the remnants of my young self—a collection I had tried and failed to refine—I found comfort in the persistence of memory. Yet, as I gazed at these familiar treasures, a strange unspoken longing twisted inside me as if each petal and brushstroke whispered secrets I had yet to uncover.

A framed photo on the bookshelf caught the moon's caress, highlighting the faces of Gini and me at ten years old with our shining hazel eyes and strawberry-blonde tresses. It stood as an impromptu bookend, its edges worn from years of being clutched in reminiscence. The innocence in our smiles belied our uncharted future. I remembered the songs we used to sing together and how Mom taught us to harmonize. We spent hours singing our hearts out. Staring at it now, a wave of nostalgia mixed with an unsettling sense of foreboding: the photograph felt like a portent, suggesting that the past was not as distant as it seemed and that some impending revelation lingered just beyond the edge of my perception.

In that room, surrounded by echoes of my childhood and the spectral silhouettes of night, I felt an uncanny blend of romance for the past and a growing unease about the unknowns that lay ahead, as if the very walls were poised to whisper secrets that would change everything.

I awoke with a jerk, my heart racing as the remnants of the dream clung to me like a cold mist. The air in the castle room was chilled, an eerie stillness enveloping me as I lay tangled in the heavy, damp linens. I tried to grasp the fleeting emotions that had surged through me in the dream—a mixture of anticipation and dread, as if I were teetering on the edge of a vast, unseen precipice.

"What did it mean?" The question echoed in the cavernous room, each whisper of sound bouncing off the ancient stone walls that hid centuries of secrets. I hadn't meant to say it aloud. I didn't want to wake anyone. A palpable sense of mystery hung in the air—as if the castle itself held memories of long-forgotten intrigues and was now speaking to me through veiled visions. I felt a compelling urge to decipher this enigma, as if understanding my dream was the key to unlocking some deeper truth hidden within these storied halls. My gaze drifted to the shadowed corners of the room, half-expecting to find an answer lurking there, watching me as I pondered the unknown.

CHAPTER TWENTY-SIX

Claire

I lay on my bed, my phone pressed against my ear, as the familiar sound of Gini's laughter filled the line. It had been weeks since we'd last spoken properly, and the comforting warmth of my sister's voice was exactly what I needed after everything that had been happening. Despite the physical distance between us, our bond was still strong—at least, that's what I kept telling myself.

"So, you've been spending all your time in the studio, huh?" Gini teased, her voice bright and playful. "Tell me you're at least eating something that isn't instant noodles."

I laughed. "Oh, I didn't tell you? The housemother here at the castle is a wonderful cook. She makes some really amazing meals. I'm well-fed. I think I've even gained some weight!" I felt along my waistline, feeling to see if there was any truth to my words. Maybe.

"Oh, I thought Mom was joking when she said that you might be dining on some interesting parts of a sheep," Gini said with a giggle.

I smiled, but there was a touch of something else—something like longing or maybe guilt—lingering in the back of my mind. Gini always seemed to have it together, always seemed so grounded. While I lost myself in my art, Gini was off excelling in everything she touched, her path clear and steady. We had always been close, but sometimes, I couldn't help but feel like I was the one trailing behind.

"So, enough about me," I said, steering the conversation away from myself. "How are things with you? Still managing to be the golden child?"

Gini groaned dramatically. "Ugh, please. If you only knew how chaotic things are right now. It's really the same old, same old."

I laughed. "Well, you can make even chaos sound so glamorous."

"Well, you know me," Gini said with a lightness that only she could pull off. "I thrive in the madness. But, seriously, how's school? Are you feeling more settled? I know it's a lot, but you've got this, Claire. You always do."

I hesitated, chewing my bottom lip. I wanted to tell Gini everything—the strange dreams, the unsettling presence of Angus, the feeling of being caught between two worlds. But how could I explain something that sounded so . . . impossible? So instead, I let out a sigh. At last, I spoke, my voice quieter. "Actually, I've been meaning to ask you something. It's kind of weird."

"Weird?" Gini's voice perked up with curiosity. "Well, now I'm interested. What's on your mind?"

I shifted, pulling my knees to my chest. "Do you . . . believe in ghosts?"

There was a pause on the other end, and I immediately regretted asking. I could almost hear the puzzled expression on Gini's face. "Ghosts? Like actual spirits?"

"Yeah," I said, feeling a bit foolish now that the words were out there. "I've been having these dreams, and they're just so real. There's this boy—Angus—and he feels like more than a dream. It's like he's actually there, like he's trying to reach me. I don't know how to explain it."

Another pause. This time, Gini's voice softened. "Are you OK, Claire? You sound . . . off."

I sighed, my fingers tightening around the phone. "I don't know. I feel like I'm losing my grip on what's real sometimes. These dreams, the way they make me feel—it's all so intense. I wake up, and I can still feel him there."

Gini was quiet for a moment, and then she spoke, her tone gentle and filled with concern. "I don't know if I believe in ghosts, but I do believe in you. And if you think there's something more going on, then maybe there is. Just don't let it consume you, OK? You've always been so good at immersing yourself in things, but sometimes that can pull you too far."

I swallowed, nodding even though Gini couldn't see me. "Yeah, I'll try. It's just hard to know what's real when everything feels blurred."

"I get it," Gini said softly. "But you're stronger than you think, Claire. You've always been. Just remember you can call me any time. Even if it's to talk about ghost Highlanders or whatever."

I chuckled, but my heart wasn't fully in it. "Thanks. I'm glad you don't think I'm completely losing it."

"You could never lose it," Gini replied warmly. "You're Claire. You're unstoppable."

We chatted for a few more minutes, the conversation returning to lighter topics, but as I hung up, a familiar heaviness settled in my chest. Gini always knew how to reassure me, to make me feel like everything was going to be OK. But even now, after our talk, I couldn't shake the sense of unease.

It wasn't just Angus and the dreams that haunted me. It was something deeper—a gnawing doubt that had followed me for years. Gini was so sure of herself, so perfect, with her seemingly effortless way of navigating life. And me, I was always questioning whether I was good enough. Good enough for my family, my dreams, for myself.

I sighed, staring at the ceiling, the echo of Gini's reassuring words still ringing in my ears. She was a good sister. And tonight, as the edges of the dreamworld blurred with my waking life, I wasn't sure which part of myself was real anymore.

Professor Stump's voice cut through the silence like a dull blade. "Claire, once again, you've completely missed the mark. This isn't abstract. It's aimless," he said, his eyes narrowing as he surveyed my sculpture. The other students exchanged glances, the sting of his words obvious.

I kept my face calm, my eyes locked on the heap of garbage known as my sculpture. Stump's disdain was hardly new to me, but today, something just felt different. The room held an edge, a subtle tension that prickled the air. Just then, the fluorescent lights overhead began to flicker, casting shadows that seemed to pulse and writhe across the walls.

"What's going on with the lights?" Julie whispered.

As Professor Stump continued his critique, his voice laced with an almost personal contempt, a loud crash came from behind him. A pile of sketchbooks had toppled from the shelf, scattering across the floor with a chaotic flourish. A collective gasp rippled through the class. The professor's face grew pale, but he brushed it off with a flustered cough.

"Settle down, everyone," he muttered, his eyes darting around the room as if expecting another disruption.

I held back a smile, my heart racing as I felt a distinct warmth, a presence beside me that only I could sense. I knew it was Angus. This was his doing. My thirteenth-century defender had a flair for the dramatic, apparently.

As Professor Stump continued his lecture, undeterred but visibly annoyed, a low rhythmic knocking sound began to emanate from the far corner of the room, seemingly from within the wall. Each thud was deliberate, almost menacing. The students exchanged nervous looks, some glancing toward the door as if ready to bolt.

Professor Stump's composure faltered, "All right, this is ridiculous. Whoever is playing these childish pranks, they will be expelled," he snapped, though there was a hint of nervousness in his tone.

I couldn't resist. I raised my hand. "Maybe it's a sign, Professor. An omen."

Stump's face flushed, and before he could respond, the lights flickered again—this time plunging the room into near darkness. A chill swept through the room. When the lights finally steadied, Professor Stump was visibly shaken, and the students sat in stunned silence, utterly bewildered. Stump dismissed class early and left the room in a blur.

Only I felt the calm assurance of Angus's presence, his silent promise to defend me, a ghostly knight from centuries past, loyal and true. I wouldn't forget.

"I'm telling you—it was a ghost. There's no other explanation. Lights flickering, books flying off the shelves—stuff like that just doesn't happen on its own." Vic took a hearty gulp of his pint and set it down with a decisive thud.

The small village pub buzzed with chatter and clinking glasses. The entire cohort huddled around our dimly lit table, eyes wide with excitement and a bit of lingering fear.

Barry, leaning back in his chair with a skeptical smirk, folded his arms. "Or maybe it's just that ancient wiring in the building finally giving out. You've all heard those creaks and groans before. The place could be deteriorating under our feet. The moisture trapped in the stone infrastructure could be compromising the whole place."

Julie leaned forward, eyes glinting. "But didn't you hear that knocking? It was like—rhythmic. Like someone was trying to make a point. And Stump's face—he was scared. The man looked like he'd seen a ghost himself!" She glanced around, grinning uncharacteristically.

I shrugged, my fingers tracing the rim of my glass as I chose my words carefully. "Well, I just think we don't know everything there is to know about old places like the castle. And sometimes, you know— maybe there are things we can't see. Things that look out for us in strange ways."

Joy, who had been mostly quiet, shivered and rubbed her arms as if warding off an invisible chill. "I just felt . . . I don't know, like we weren't alone. I was sure something was there, and it didn't feel like it wanted us to stay. Especially Stump. Remember what Effie told us? Lady Red? The laird?"

Vic leaned in, his voice dropping to a whisper. "Stump's disrupted the spirits."

I fought to keep a straight face. Angus, I thought, had certainly left an impression.

Barry let out a scoff. "Please. Come on. If anything, it was probably one of you lot messing around to get a reaction out of old Stump." He glanced at me with a grin. "Or maybe Claire here's got some secret powers she's hiding."

I laughed, shaking my head. "If I had ghost powers, Barry, don't you think I'd use them for something a bit more productive?"

The cohort laughed, but I noticed the others casting glances my way, curiosity obviously piqued. I raised my glass, and they all followed suit, clinking the glasses together.

"To the mystery of the castle," I said, "And to all the things we may never fully understand."

The others drank, murmuring toasts and laughter, but I sensed the faintest whisper, lingering in the shadows, watchful as ever.

CHAPTER TWENTY-SEVEN

Claire

I sat across from Joy in the empty dining hall of the castle, stirring my tea. "OK, Joy," I began, feeling a grin seize my expression. "How many boyfriends have you actually had?"

Joy snorted, nearly spilling her coffee. "Well, let's just say if my love life were an art exhibit, it would be minimalism," she quipped, laughing. "What about you? You're young but very pretty. I bet you have a story or two to tell, right?"

I leaned back with a sigh. "If by 'story,' you mean short story, then you are right. My longest relationship lasted three months, and one of those was during Christmas break."

Joy's eyes sparkled with amusement. "Ah, the infamous holiday relationship! Did he know he was dating you, or was he just a muse who walked by at the wrong time?"

I laughed. "We grew up together, and I always had a crush on him. But one day, he decided I was, you know, the mysterious and oh-so-cool 'art girl.' In reality, I just needed to figure out if the idea of him was what I liked most." I fidgeted with my diamond bracelet absentmindedly.

Joy nodded. "Classic rookie mistake. I once thought I liked this guy because he always smelled like coffee and cinnamon. Turned out, I just really like coffee and cinnamon."

We both burst into laughter.

"So, here we are, two sophisticated, cultured young women with almost zero experience in the boyfriend department . . ."

Joy laughed. "Hey, at least we're saving all that energy for the right guys—or, you know, for making more art."

"Exactly." I grinned. "After all, boys are temporary, but art is forever."

As Joy and I walked back to the art studio, the eternally cool air in the castle moved around me, the musty smell vaguely noticeable now, stirring thoughts I tried to keep at bay. Angus—the ghost from my dreams. How had my mind conjured him so vividly? His face, his voice, the way he spoke with such eloquence, and his laugh—it all felt so real.

I shook my head, giving myself a wry smile. *A ghost, Claire,* I thought. *You're getting worked up over someone who doesn't even exist.* But despite myself, I felt a pang—a longing that felt too deep for something born purely of imagination.

The truth, though I hated to admit it, was that Angus felt more genuine than any of the quick romances I'd tried to find with boys who were, well, actually alive. In my dreams, I felt truly seen by him. Angus made my heart race and seemed to understand my perception of the world through my art. In a way, he was exactly what I wished I could find. If only he weren't separated from me by centuries and the inexplicable veil of dreams.

I sighed, turning the corner down the hallway, realizing Joy had been chattering the entire way. *You're falling for a ghost,* I thought with a shake of my head. *Even if he were real, he belongs to a past that's gone. It's impossible, ridiculous.*

But still, part of me felt incomplete without him.

CHAPTER TWENTY-EIGHT

Kaya

K aya sat across from May, her eyes a little wider than usual. "I had a chat with Gini about Claire last night," Kaya began, voice tinged with worry. "Gini seems to think Claire's been acting odd since she started studying in your castle. She's convinced the place is haunted."

May snorted, half-laughing, half-sighing. "Haunted? Kaya, the entire country of Scotland is haunted. You can't walk ten feet without hearing about some ghost or another." She gave a teasing grin. "What did Gini think was going to happen? Claire's studying in a castle. Of course, there'll be a ghost or two!"

Kaya frowned, stirring her tea absently. "But it's not just the castle, May. Claire seems so distant lately. And she's been dreaming about some medieval ghost."

"Ha! I bet he's got a good, strong name too!" May chuckled, a glint of amusement in her eyes. "A Scottish ghost invading Claire's dreams. A handsome Highlander, I'm sure. Claire's a lucky lass!"

Kaya gave her sister a look—part exasperation and part amusement. "I'm being serious, May! I've been having my own dreams. Actually, nightmares. And in them, I can't find Claire. I've been having this feeling that I need to warn her about something, but I don't know what. What if it's this ghost I'm supposed to warn her about? But more practically, what if this ghost is affecting her sleep or her studies? I'm trying not to be crazy about this, but . . ."

May reached across the table, placing a gentle hand on Kaya's. "Look, Kiki, Claire's in Scotland, one of the oldest, most mystical places you could imagine. If she's feeling inspired by a little haunting, maybe it's the creative spark she's needed all along. Besides, wouldn't you say it's a little romantic?"

Kaya chuckled in spite of herself. "Romantic? My daughter in love with a ghost?"

May grinned. "There are worse suitors, and let's face it: a medieval ghost isn't likely to whisk her away to the Highlands anytime soon."

Kaya took a deep breath, finally smiling. "You're right. Maybe I need to trust Claire to figure this out. She's got a good head on her shoulders, even if it's full of castles and ghosts."

"Exactly," May said, taking a bite of scone. "I'm a little jealous, actually. A ghost sounds like the perfect beau at my age. I mean, no cooking, no laundry. Come on, Kiki!"

Kaya laughed, relaxing a bit.

"But seriously, if this ghostly influence keeps Claire inspired, it can't be all bad."

"I mean, you spent time at that castle before you bought it. You would've known if it felt unsettling."

"Yes. I bought it with plasma gun in hand, ready to destroy any nasty ghouls that lurked," May joked.

"OK, yes. I sound ridiculous."

"It felt like a wonderfully mystical old place. That's why I bought it. I never had any bad vibes while I was there."

"OK. I'll take your word for it." Kaya finished her tea, hoping that she was indeed being ridiculous. "I'll try to stop worrying."

CHAPTER TWENTY-NINE

Claire

In my dream, I found myself in a grand, candlelit hall that seemed to shimmer with a soft, golden glow. I wore a deep sapphire blue dress, the fabric whispering around me as I moved, and there before me was Angus, his gaze warm and intense, as if I were the only soul he'd ever seen. His hand reached out, strong and gentle, inviting me to dance.

As he drew me close, our movements became as natural as breathing, our steps effortless and in perfect harmony. The music, ethereal and ancient, wove around us, a melody that seemed to belong to another world—a world where time, distance, even life and death had no power over love.

Angus looked down at me, his hand resting lightly on my waist. "I've waited lifetimes to see ye," he whispered, his voice a low murmur that seemed to brush against my heart. My own breath caught, my hand tightening in his as we spun, my dress fanning out in a swirl of deep blue against the glowing light.

In that moment, every worry and every thought of the waking world faded, replaced only by the soft brush of his hand, the gentle warmth of his eyes, and the unspoken promise lingering between us. I could feel the edges of the dream beginning to blur, reality beginning to press in, but I clung to him, desperate for just a few more precious moments. I wished with everything in my heart that I could somehow stay, that I could break the impossible barriers that separated us.

"Claire," he said, his voice like a balm and a wound all at once. His gaze softened, filled with a sadness that mirrored my feelings. "I would cross every boundary of time, of life, for you, but this dance must end."

I felt myself fading, but before the dream slipped completely, I closed my eyes, pressing my hand in his and whispering, "Then find me, Angus. In whatever way you can, find me."

As I awoke, a tear slipped down my cheek, and for a moment, it felt as though I could still feel the warmth of his hand in mine, the lingering echo of our dance holding my heart tightly in its grip.

CHAPTER THIRTY

Claire

The air in Professor Stump's studio felt thick, almost stifling. High ceilings and tall, narrow windows gave the room a chilly feel and matched the stony expression on Stump's face as he continued his long-winded lecture. His words filled the room like a heavy fog, each sentence dragged out with exaggerated, self-important pauses.

"And as I have reiterated countless times," he droned, his voice carrying a theatrical flair, "true artistry is not about imitation—it's about transcendence, the rise from mere skill to sublime creation. Which, as many of you have yet to grasp, is a process that takes more than a mere few years to comprehend. Some of you, no doubt, may never rise to such heights."

I sat toward the back, hands gripping my sketchbook tightly, my knuckles pale against the paper. My gaze remained on the stone floor. Each word Stump spoke coiled around my heart like a tightening vice. I could feel him looking my way, his eyes burning with a particular sharpness whenever he spoke of "true artists" or made disparaging remarks about "young, untested talent." Though he didn't mention my name, the meaning was clear enough.

My cohort shifted in their seats, exchanging tired, sympathetic glances. The others were equally bored and restless, but I could tell that they felt the tension too. They all had affirmed Stump had a particular disdain for me, and each lecture seemed to drag on with extra bite aimed in my direction.

Just when I thought I couldn't bear another minute, Stump's monologue came to a sudden end. He pursed his lips, glancing around the room with a contemptuous sneer. "I expect your projects to demonstrate more than the expected, more than the average. Do not disappoint me. Class dismissed."

I let out a breath, hoping that maybe, for once, I'd make it out without a confrontation. I gathered my things quickly, trying to avoid eye contact as I stood. But just as I turned toward the door, a shadow loomed in my path. I looked up to find Professor Stump standing before me, his eyes narrowed, a wry, almost malicious smile on his lips.

"Mizz Boucher," he drawled, voice low and mocking, "I hope you're not under the impression that your lineage will earn you special treatment in my class."

My stomach twisted. I swallowed, trying to keep my voice steady. "I wouldn't expect any special treatment, Professor."

"Good," he replied, his smile tightening. "You see, it's one thing to carry the weight of family privilege, but it's quite another to be deserving of it. Your Aunt May may own this castle, but in my classroom, I am the authority. And rest assured," he leaned in, his voice barely above a whisper, "I will not let you coast by with mediocrity simply because you come from money."

His words cut deep, but I stood my ground, though my hands trembled slightly. Stump's eyes flashed with satisfaction at my discomfort, his tone becoming sharper. "You're the youngest student in this program, obviously. Quite frankly, I doubt you have the skill to finish with any merit. I would suggest you prepare yourself for the very real possibility that you may fail this class."

Jaw clenched, I tried to not let fear show in my eyes. But Stump just straightened, a gleam of satisfaction flickering in his gaze. "After all, Mizz Boucher, sometimes failure is the best teacher." With that, he gave a curt nod and turned, leaving me alone in the now-empty studio, his words echoing in the quiet as I stood, motionless, my heart pounding in my ears.

As I stepped out of the studio, still reeling from my tense encounter with Professor Stump, I almost walked right past Vic, who was leaning against the stone wall just outside the door. His sandy-colored hair was slightly mussed, and his brow furrowed with a look of quiet determination as he caught my eye.

"Hey, Claire," he said, his voice low but warm. "You OK? I saw him corner you in there."

I managed to nod, though I couldn't completely mask the frustration and exhaustion I felt. "Yeah, it's just Stump. You know how he is."

Vic shook his head, letting out a sigh. "Yeah, too well." He hesitated for a moment, then leaned in closer, glancing around to make sure no one else was nearby. "Listen, some of us in the cohort have been talking. We're considering filing a grievance against him for, well . . . everything. The intimidation, the constant humiliation. It's way out of line, and we're done putting up with it."

My eyes widened slightly, I'd heard my classmates whisper about Stump's attitude before, but I hadn't realized there was enough momentum for an actual complaint. "You think it'll work? He's been with the university for ages."

Vic shrugged, though there was a spark of hope in his eyes. "Maybe. It depends on whether enough of us are willing to sign on. But I've seen him single you out more than anyone, Claire. If you spoke up, it might help make our case stronger."

I took a deep breath, considering his words. I'd dreamed of standing up to Stump, of letting him know how deeply his words had cut, how his relentless criticisms felt like a constant weight pressing down on me. But the idea of actually doing it—of officially challenging him—felt like stepping into unknown, turbulent waters.

"Are you sure this is a good idea?" I asked, glancing down the empty hallway, half-expecting Stump to appear again.

Vic nodded firmly. "Claire, we can't keep letting him get away with this. He shouldn't have that kind of power over us. We're here to learn, to create, not to be torn down."

I studied his expression, finding strength in his resolve. "OK," I whispered, my voice gaining steadiness. "I'll join you. Let's put this grievance together."

Vic's face broke into a relieved smile, and he gave me a small, encouraging nod. "Great. Let's meet with the others and go over everything. We're going to need all the support we can get, and your voice is going to mean a lot to them."

For the first time that day, I felt a glimmer of hope. As I walked beside Vic down the corridor, I couldn't help but feel that maybe, just maybe, we could do this. Maybe we could take back our courage, our creativity, and make the studio a place where we could finally thrive.

Though we were so far apart, the phone connection with my mom was crystal clear. Amazing, really. My mom's voice sounded so near that I felt grounded with a sense of home I'd not realized I missed so much.

"Hi, sweetheart," my mom's voice was soft, soothing. "How's everything going over there? You sounded a little off last time we spoke."

I took a breath, then found myself smiling. "Actually, things are looking up, Mom," I replied. The weight that had clung to me since I arrived at the castle finally started to lift. "I mean, it's not all easy. Professor Stump has been . . . difficult. Really difficult, actually. But—" I hesitated, realizing I didn't want to dwell on him. "But something good's come of it too."

"Good? Tell me everything," Mom said, a smile audible in her voice.

"Well, a few of my classmates are talking about taking a stand against Stump's, uh, teaching style." I laughed lightly, then added, "He's intense, to put it mildly. But I think it's actually brought me closer to everyone. We're kind of in this together."

Mom let out a small, thoughtful hum. "You know, sometimes the toughest situations help you find your people. Maybe it's not exactly what you expected, but I'm glad you're finding support there, honey. And it sounds like you're handling it really well."

I felt a little rush of pride. "Thanks, Mom. And, well, I've been finding inspiration in places I didn't expect either. There's something about being here, with all this history, that makes me feel connected. Like I'm part of something bigger."

My mom's voice softened. "I'm so proud of you, Claire. You've always had such a beautiful heart for art and a way of connecting to the world. I know it hasn't been easy, but it sounds like you're finding your way."

"Yeah," I agreed, feeling warmth bloom in my chest. "I am. Slowly, but I am." I paused, then added, "I guess I didn't realize how much I'd love it here, even with all the challenges."

We chatted a few more minutes, and as we said our goodbyes, I felt a renewed sense of purpose, knowing my mom was there for me, cheering me on from across the world.

CHAPTER THIRTY-ONE

EXCERPT FROM DIORVAL

He led me to the landing, the air growing colder as we approached the base of the staircase. With a fluid, almost theatrical gesture, he waved his hand, and to my disbelief, the stones of the wall slid away silently, revealing a ghastly hidden chamber. My breath caught in my throat as the dim light fell upon the skeletal remains, each frozen in an eternal plea for mercy, their palms outstretched as if to push away their cruel fate. The realization of what I was seeing struck me like a physical blow—these souls had been walled in, left to a torturous end within the confines of this very castle.

Diorval's voice, heavy with a somber gravity, broke the prolonged silence, "They were walled in alive."

His words echoed ominously through the stone corridor, amplifying the horror of the revelation. But it was the sight at the feet of one skeleton that rooted me to the spot—a smaller, more delicate set of bones, unmistakably those of an infant. A tiny life snuffed out in this dark tomb.

"He was a monster," I managed to say, my voice trembling as the chilling truth settled in.

"He is the spirit that haunts this place. His curse has me trapped here," he continued, his tone grave. "You and I would have enough power together to defeat him."

"What do you mean 'defeat him?' He's a ghost, right?" I stammered, the panic rising in me like a tide, threatening to overwhelm my senses.

"He's more than just a ghost," Diorval replied, his voice a whisper that seemed to blend with the shadows that danced on the walls. "He's a malevolent force tied to this castle, feeding on the despair of the trapped and the lost. He's why I can't leave. And now, he knows you know."

The air round us pulsed as if alive. The spectral moans of the entombed seemed to seep from the walls, a lament for their unjust end and a chilling warning of the fate that could befall me if I lingered too long in this cursed place. The horror of my discovery weighed heavily upon me, a tangible dread that urged me to flee before I, too, became a permanent resident of this haunted fortress.

CHAPTER THIRTY-TWO

Claire

The night air was cool, scented with a hint of wild heather and something that whispered of forgotten times. Stars stretched endlessly above, casting a faint silver glow over the landscape, illuminating each blade of grass and soft shadow. I walked beside Angus, my hand nestled in the crook of his arm, feeling the warmth radiating from him in a way that seemed impossible yet achingly real.

He was quiet, his gaze on the horizon, but every so often, his eyes would flicker toward me, filled with a depth and tenderness that sent a thrill through my heart. The silence between us was comfortable, charged with an understanding that needed no words.

We stopped at the crest of a hill, looking out over a view so breathtaking it stole the air from my lungs. Stars reflected in a dark, glassy lake below, each point of light mirrored like a thousand fireflies caught in the water's surface. Angus turned to me, his gaze soft and searching.

"Does this feel like a dream to you, Claire?" he asked, his voice low, a touch of sadness lacing his words.

I took a shivering breath, unable to look away from him. "No. It feels more real than anything else. It's like I've been waiting for this, for you, without even knowing it." My voice faltered, but I couldn't stop myself from speaking the truth.

He reached up, brushing a lock of hair from my face, his touch feather-light but as tangible as the earth beneath my feet. "Aye, lass. That's the trouble, isn't it? I feel as real to you as you do to me, but when the sun rises . . ." His voice trailed off, and I could see the same anguish I felt reflected in his eyes.

I pressed my hand to his chest, feeling his heart beneath my fingertips, torn between the dreamscape and the waking world. "Angus, what if—what if this is the real world? What if everything else, my studies, my life—what if that's the dream?" My voice was barely a whisper, the words escaping before I could stop them.

He held my gaze, his expression solemn yet touched by a soft, wistful smile. "If that were true, I'd be the happiest soul who ever walked this land," he murmured, his hand lingering on mine, his touch binding me to the moment.

We stood there, lost in each other's eyes, feeling the vastness of time slip away. I knew that soon I'd wake, and this world would dissolve into morning light. But a part of my heart was starting to wonder if I'd ever truly be at home in that waking world again. For here, beneath the stars beside him, I felt as if I'd found a piece of myself I hadn't known was missing.

This must be what falling in love felt like.

⌘

The rest of our classmates had gone to the pub, but Joy and I stayed behind. We were comfy and cozy in our pajamas, sitting on our beds. Joy sat across from me, her eyes bright with interest as I hesitated, staring down at my hands and struggling to find the right words.

"Joy, there's something I want to tell you. I've only told my sister about it, and I need another perspective, if possible," I began, my voice barely above a whisper. "It sounds impossible, but I think you might understand."

Joy leaned forward, her expression open and encouraging. "Hey, whatever it is, I'm here. You can trust me."

Taking a deep breath, I plunged in. "I've been having these dreams. But they're more than dreams—they feel so real, like I'm actually there. And in these dreams, I'm with someone. His name is Angus."

Joy's eyebrows lifted slightly, but she said nothing, just nodded for me to continue.

"He's from another time—medieval Scotland," I said, my voice dimming as if speaking my experience aloud might make it vanish. "We talk, and sometimes we walk together under the stars. The other night, we even danced. I know it's impossible. I know he's a ghost. But when I'm with him, it doesn't feel like a dream. It feels like it's the most real thing I've ever experienced."

Joy's face softened with a mix of awe and compassion. "That sounds incredible, Claire. Beautiful, even. But I can see how it might be hard too."

I nodded, fidgeting all the while with my bracelet. "It is. Every time I wake up, it feels like I'm leaving him behind. I get this terrible, empty feeling, like I'm being pulled between two worlds. When I'm awake, I'm here, with you, with my classes, my life. But then, there's this other part of me that feels like it belongs there, with him."

Joy reached over to me, brushing a few strands of hair away from my eyes. s "That's a lot to carry. Have you thought about what these dreams could mean? Maybe it's something you need to explore, even if just to understand why it's so powerful for you."

I sighed, feeling a mixture of hope and sorrow. "I have thought about it, but every answer I come up with feels so distant. I don't want to give up on him, but I don't know if he's real. Or if he's just some part of my imagination."

Joy sighed while giving a small shrug. "Maybe it doesn't have to be one or the other. Maybe Angus and these dreams are showing you a part of yourself you didn't know was there. Something meaningful, whether he's ghost or just . . . well, a beautiful soul. Whatever the truth is, I'll be here for you, OK?"

A grateful smile broke out across my face. "Thank you, Joy. I didn't realize how much I needed to talk about this. I'm so lucky to have you."

Joy grinned back, her eyes warm. "That's what friends are for, Claire. Just promise me that if Angus invites you to a medieval ball, you'll tell me every detail."

We both laughed, and for the first time in days, I felt a little lighter, knowing I wasn't carrying this alone.

CHAPTER THIRTY-THREE

Kaya

The sun shone brightly over Kaya and Cole's backyard. A few of the family gathered for a long-awaited summer afternoon by the pool. Laughter and conversation flowed easily, mingling with the scent of sunscreen and the sweet tang of strawberry daiquiris that Kaya had expertly whipped up. Livy and May sat side by side, stretching out on lounge chairs and sipping their drinks, while Livy's triplets—Heather, Hazel, and Holly—were sprawled on brightly colored towels nearby, flipping through magazines and stealing sips from their mom's drink when she wasn't looking.

"Oh, I swear"—Livy laughed, watching her girls—"it feels like just yesterday when you three were running around in those matching swimsuits with the frilly bottoms."

The triplets rolled their eyes but smiled, clearly used to the family nostalgia. Hazel, the quietest of the three nudged Heather and grinned. "Maybe we should have gone with the frills today—seems to be Mom's favorite look."

"Don't you dare." Livy chuckled, shaking her head. "One trip down memory lane is enough."

Ivy, seated gracefully under a large sunhat and sunglasses that made her look every bit the queen of the poolside, let out a warm laugh. "You girls have grown so fast. It's hard keeping up with all of you."

May glanced over at Kaya. "I can't help but think of Claire and Gini," she said with a wistful smile. "It feels strange not having those two running around here with you all. I swear every time I look at them, they're more grown up than before."

Kaya's expression turned sentimental, and she nodded. "It does feel strange. They're off having their own adventures now, but sometimes I just want to keep them right here. Claire's in Scotland, immersed in art, and Gini's so focused on her studies too. I'm so proud of them, but I miss them."

Holly, who had been listening with a knowing smile, piped up, "I'll bet Claire is absolutely loving it in Scotland, though. All those castles and art classes—it's like something out of a storybook."

Livy laughed. "You've always been romantic, Holly. But I think you're right—if there's anyone who'd fall in love with ancient castles, it's Claire."

"And Gini's just as special," Ivy chimed in, her gaze warm with grandmotherly pride. "I know she's got her hands full with her own studies, but that girl has her heart in the right place. Just like all of you."

Kaya sighed, taking in the scene, the laughter, the love that filled her backyard. "It's a blessing to have moments like these, isn't it? Even when they're off on their own, I know they'll come back to us. Summers like this are a reminder that family is always home."

As the afternoon wore on, the women fell back into light-hearted chatter, swapping funny family memories, laughing at old jokes, and sharing memories of summers past and hopes of those yet to come. In that golden, sunlit space, Kaya felt whole, bound to the others by laughter, love, and a lingering sense of togetherness that would follow them wherever life took them next.

CHAPTER THIRTY-FOUR

Claire

I woke slowly, lingering in that fragile space between sleep and waking, where reality felt thin, where my mind could almost convince myself that the dream had been real. My fingers reached out instinctively, as though I could still feel the warmth of Angus's hand, the faint scent of pine and woodsmoke that seemed to linger whenever he was near. But as my eyes opened fully, I was met only with the soft, familiar darkness of my room.

I sat up, pulling the blanket around my shoulders, and tried to hold on to the details of the dream before they drifted away. His voice, the way he looked at me under that endless expanse of stars—it was all still so vivid. He felt more than real—woven into my very being. How was it possible to feel so much for someone who didn't belong to my world, my time?

I sighed, pressing a hand to my chest. This dream felt different. Deeper, somehow. Each time I saw Angus, each night we spent talking, walking, dancing, I felt something shift inside me, a part of myself I hadn't even realized was missing until now. And now? I didn't know what to do with it. It was like I was caught between two lives—the one I knew and this weird connection that made no sense but felt real anyway.

I turned my gaze to the soft light filtering in, wondering, *What am I supposed to do with this?* There was no answer, no roadmap that would explain what I was feeling, and certainly no simple choice. Was Angus a reflection of some part of myself I hadn't yet understood, an echo from another life, or something beyond even my imagination?

I lay back down, staring at the dark, shadowed ceiling. The experiences felt like pieces of a puzzle, scattered and strange, yet somehow linked. I couldn't quite make out the image they formed, but the shapes and edges seemed to invite me to try. Maybe it was a challenge, a question posed by the universe itself, inviting me to stretch beyond my assumptions and fears to look deeper within myself.

My heart felt heavy yet full, alive in a way that was both exhilarating and unsettling. I'd always seen myself as grounded, sensible, yet these dreams awakened something wild and free within me, a longing for something I couldn't even name.

"What if I'm missing something about who I really am?" I asked myself, silently, half-wishing Angus were there to answer me. "What if this isn't just a dream? What if it's more?"

Again, I didn't have an answer, but I felt something shift inside me as I considered the possibilities. Maybe, for now, it was enough to explore, to open myself to the vastness of the unknown. Life didn't always need definitive answers. Sometimes, it was enough to walk the path without seeing the end, to accept the mystery without unraveling it.

I closed my eyes again, feeling a calm settle over me. Angus might be a dream, or he might be something more than that. But as I drifted in that gentle twilight of thought, I knew I was ready to discover whatever the universe held in store—one step, one question, one dream at a time.

CHAPTER THIRTY-FIVE

Claire

The eight of us sat huddled together in one of the castle's small, dimly lit study rooms. The atmosphere was charged with a mixture of tension and determination as we passed around a makeshift petition, a single sheet of paper with the carefully worded grievance against Professor Stump. The air smelled faintly of old parchment and coffee, and our voices echoed in the stone-walled room as each of us took turns speaking.

Vic, who had spearheaded the idea, broke the silence. "Look, we've all been through it with Stump—his insults, the way he singles us out just to tear us down. It's not right. We're here to learn, to create, not to be picked apart for his amusement." His voice was resolute, and he glanced around the group, his gaze settling on each person with encouragement.

Barry nodded. "I thought I was enough to be here at the start, but the feedback Stump has been giving me has really shaken my confidence."

Joy leaned forward, her voice soft yet laced with frustration and conviction. "It's almost as if he's trying to see how far he can push us before we break. But we didn't come all this way, to this beautiful place, just to be bullied out of our passion for art."

Julie added, "I thought about leaving. Honestly, after the last class, I was ready to pack my bags. But that's not fair. I deserve to be here."

Glancing my way, she added, "We all deserve to be here. If this petition can make things better for us, I'll sign."

I sat up straighter, feeling a swell of solidarity. "We can't let him undermine our confidence like this. I think we've all had enough. I'm in too." My voice was firm, though I could feel the weight of my earlier interactions with Stump bearing down on me. Still, the support of the cohort gave me strength.

Rob chimed in with a grin, "I knew the guy was insufferable, but if he's got us all thinking of giving up? Yeah, that's a problem. Count me in. I'm tired of feeling like I'm constantly under attack."

Tiffany gave a determined nod. "He's always talking about 'real artists' as if we're just amateurs he has to tolerate. But we're here because we have something to offer too. I want this to be a place where we can actually grow, not where we're afraid to try."

Carissa, who had been listening intently, finally spoke up, her voice filled with emotion. "I love this place, this castle, the history, all of it. But every time I step into his class, I feel like I lose a bit of myself. I'm not willing to keep giving that up. I'll sign."

Vic took a deep breath, his eyes shining with pride and relief. "Then it's settled. We're doing this together." He set the petition on the table, pushing it toward the group with a sense of finality.

One by one, my cohort picked up the pen and signed their names, the ink marking a stand not just against Professor Stump but for each other. When it was my turn, I felt a wave of courage wash over me as I put pen to paper. We were all different, each with our unique style and voice, but in that moment, we were united as one.

As the last signature was added, Vic carefully folded the paper. "Tomorrow, I'll send this to the department head. It's time someone knows what's going on in that classroom."

We all exchanged glances, a silent bond forming among us—a shared promise to see this through.

CHAPTER THIRTY-SIX

EXCERPT FROM DIORVAL

As the autumn sun dipped below the horizon, casting shadows across the castle's stone corridors, I sat at my desk, pen in hand, recording the most recent of my peculiar encounters with Diorval. A draft brushed against my cheek, familiar now, like the sweep of his fingers, and I glanced up to find him there, a shimmer in the twilight, his form as ethereal as a distant memory. His dark eyes held that knowing glint—an unspoken promise between us that had woven itself into the very fabric of my life here.

For months, I'd been grappling with what he was, the mystery of his past, and the strangeness of our connection. In the beginning, it was fascination—he was a curiosity, a relic of a time lost. But now, as I sat there, the soft scratch of my pen fading into silence, I understood with sudden, alarming clarity.

My internal conflict grew with each day.

I had fallen in love with him. Not just the enigma of his ghostly presence or the thrill of his timeless charm, but with him—his dedicated and passionate heart for his mission, his warmth, the kindness that defied his spectral state.

Diorval, bound to the shadows of this place, was everything I should have resisted. A man of ancient secrets and tragedies, tethered to a realm beyond my reach. Yet his touch, insubstantial as mist, had found its way into my heart, filling the quiet spaces with a longing that no mortal could satisfy. In the depth of night, when all else had faded, it was his voice that lingered, his face I saw.

My hand stilled over the paper, and I closed my eyes, letting the truth settle over me. Loving him would never be simple. There would be no future, no earthly embrace to bridge the gap between our worlds. But what I felt was undeniable, and as impossible as it seemed, I would carry this love as I would a flame in the dark, fiercely and without regret.

CHAPTER THIRTY-SEVEN

Claire

The air was thick with unspoken tension as I shuffled into Stump's classroom with my cohort all around me. We exchanged nervous glances with each other. The strange smell of our trash sculptures filled the room. I couldn't wait for this project to be over, and today was the anticipated last day of it. I wondered if Professor Stump had been notified about the grievance yet—the letter may have been delivered to him this morning if everything was on time. The girls in my room had spent ample time last night dreadfully imagining aloud how he might respond. No one had slept well.

When Stump finally strode in, the room seemed to grow colder. His silence was sharper than any words he could have chosen. Shrewd eyes swept across us with a look acidic enough to curdle milk. He took his place at the front of the class, his fingers steepled, a slight smirk curling at the corners of his mouth.

"Today," he began, his voice like gravel over glass, "we will not be discussing anything trivial. No, I expect only the most serious of efforts today. After all," he said, eyes locking on mine, "we will complete our sculptures today, no matter how they turn out."

My pulse quickened, but I held his gaze, refusing to let him see me flinch. I could feel Joy tensing beside me, shoulders stiff, and the others' breath seemed to come more shallowly as we waited for him to continue.

He had given us an assignment—a difficult one, designed to press every one of our limits. We had each crafted a sizable abstract sculpture made of trash. "Let's see how we finish today," he said, crossing his arms and leaning against the wall with a cold smile.

The hours that followed were a test in every way. Not just of skill but of resilience. His presence was a constant weight behind us as he stalked through the aisles, watching us work with a disapproving frown or delivering thinly veiled insults about our techniques. My hands were sore, muscles strained, yet I forced myself to keep going, matching his challenge with quiet determination. I could feel the same grit from my classmates. We would not let him intimidate us, no matter how much he tried to break us down.

As the class finally ended, he dismissed us with a nod, eyes still gleaming with that sense of barely contained malice. But as I packed up my tools, I felt a new resolve brewing within me. He might hold us in this tense grip for now, but I knew that together, we would find a way to make him answer for his behavior—no matter how many of these "tests" he threw in our path.

The hum of conversation and clinking glasses filled the warm air of the pub, which felt worlds away from the cold weight of Professor Stump's studio. My classmates and I had claimed a booth near the fireplace, where we huddled close. Each drink offered a balm against the nerves still vibrating from the day's ordeal.

Julie was the first to speak, swirling her drink and staring into the amber depths as if they might offer her some comfort. "He was . . . horrible. It felt like he was just waiting for any one of us to crack," she said, her voice tight with frustration. "I swear he was enjoying it."

Heads nodded in solemn agreement, each of us still feeling the sting of Stump's scornful gaze and biting remarks.

I sipped my ginger ale, Stump's scathing comments echoing in my head. What an unhappy troll he was.

Barry leaned back in his seat, rubbing his temples. "I know he can be bad, but today? He was a different level. I felt like I could barely breathe without him watching me, waiting for me to mess up."

"What do you think he'll do?" Joy asked, her voice barely a whisper. Her hands were knotted around her can of ginger ale, knuckles white.

I glanced around, catching the unease in all their faces. "I don't know, but he won't let it slide quietly. Stump thrives on having control. He's already trying to rattle us, and he'll keep pushing until one of us gives in."

We sat in silence for a moment, each of us wrapped in the uncertainty of it. It was Vic who finally broke the quiet, letting out a small, rueful laugh. "This is exactly what he wants. He wants us to feel this way—on edge, afraid, questioning ourselves."

"You're right," I said, a spark of anger flaring in my chest. "And he'll use every chance he gets to make us feel small. But we filed the grievance for a reason. If we back down now, we're just giving him permission to keep treating us like this."

They all looked at me, the weight of our shared determination uniting us. I could feel the resolve building, a solidarity that had taken root over these last difficult months. We weren't just classmates anymore—we were allies.

Julie proclaimed with a glint of defiance in her eyes, "We're standing up to Professor Stump. We'll make him wish he'd been a janitor."

A chuckle followed by murmurs of agreement flowed around the table, a small but fierce act of rebellion.

As we left the pub, laughter mingling with the cool night air, I absently touched my wrist, feeling for the familiar weight of my diamond bracelet. My fingers met bare skin, and a sharp pang of worry struck me—this wasn't the first time it had slipped off. I stopped, calling after everyone, "Guys! I think I left my bracelet inside. Go on ahead. I'll catch up."

They waved me off, their voices fading as they continued on toward the castle. I slipped back into the pub, weaving between the remaining patrons, my eyes scanning the floor near the booth where we'd been sitting. Relief washed over me as I spotted the bracelet glinting under the table, a tiny shimmer of starlight against the wood. I scooped it up, fastening it more securely this time, and turned to leave.

Outside, the world hushed, the cobblestone street leading back to the castle was shrouded in mist. The laughter and warmth of the pub now felt far away, replaced by the unsettling silence of the deserted path. The unusual absence of wind felt bothersome now. My footsteps echoed, the sound bouncing off the darkened buildings, and each shadow seemed to grow, reaching out as I passed.

The castle loomed in the distance, its turrets sharp against the twilight sky. I shivered, pulling my sweater around my shoulders as I walked, my breaths shallow. As I neared, my gaze drifted up to the windows, their dark panes blank and empty—or so I thought. My heart skipped as a figure flickered into view, standing still in the window of one of the upper rooms.

I froze, feeling the blood draining from my face. The figure was dressed in a flowing gown, its color unmistakably crimson. I remembered Effie's story about Lady Red, the tragic spirit who haunted the castle, said to wander its halls, protecting the laird's treasure. Most of my cohort passed it off as just a story, a dramatic legend to give the castle a certain charm. But standing there alone, with Lady Red's hollow gaze seemingly fixed on me, I felt my courage waver.

The figure shifted slightly, then vanished as quickly as it had appeared, leaving only the faintest trace of red in the shadows. My heart pounded, my skin prickling with a chill deeper than the night air could account for. I hurried forward, my feet moving of their own accord, my eyes cast down to avoid the windows. But as I reached the castle's entrance, I dared a glance over my shoulder, half-expecting to see Lady Red still watching me.

The night was empty, silent once more, but something lingered—a feeling that I'd been seen, watched by eyes that had stared through centuries, perhaps sharing my sorrow, my longing. I took a shaky breath and slipped inside, vowing to keep the encounter to myself. Some things, I thought, were best left unspoken.

CHAPTER THIRTY-EIGHT

Claire

I stepped into the kitchen, drawn by the scent of freshly baked scones and the comforting hum of conversation. I stopped in my tracks, blinking in disbelief at the scene before me: Aunt May and Effie were perched at the table, each with a spoon balanced precariously on her nose, giggling like schoolgirls. Aunt May had kept her word to visit her castle while I was studying here and she had no idea how happy I was to see her, sitting in the kitchen at this moment.

"Claire, my darling!" Aunt May said when she noticed me standing in the doorway, her spoon clattering onto the table. "Come join us! Effie claims she can keep hers up longer than I can, but I'm convinced she's cheating."

"I've got a perfectly straight nose, May." Effie gave a wink and carefully rebalanced her spoon. "It's not my fault I've been blessed with superior spoon-hanging skills."

I smiled and shook my head as I moved closer to these silver-haired beauties. "I think I've walked into some sort of parallel universe. Since when are spoon-related talents part of castle life?"

"Since forever, lass," Effie said with mock seriousness, plucking the spoon off her nose and gesturing me to sit. "This castle needs a bit of silliness now and then. Keeps the ghosts in check."

May poured me a cup of tea, then slid a plate of scones my way. "You're always so serious, Claire. You should try it sometime—balancing a spoon on your nose is surprisingly enlightening."

I chuckled, remembering how Gini and I used to entertain ourselves with that very pastime. "Enlightening?" I echoed, arching my brow in a moment of skepticism as I reached for a scone. "Is this what you two have been doing while I've been trying to survive Professor Stump's artistic gauntlet?"

May and Effie shared a conspiratorial glance, their laughter softening into fond smiles. May leaned forward, resting her chin in her hand. "Claire, darling, life isn't just about surviving. It's about living. Laughing. Taking time to do ridiculous things like this, even when the world feels impossibly heavy."

Effie nodded, her warm, motherly gaze meeting mine. "And that applies to more than just our art, dear. When's the last time you let yourself truly enjoy something—or someone—without worrying about what's next?"

I hesitated, suddenly feeling the weight of their words. I thought of my whirlwind of emotions around Angus, of my uncertainty and hesitation about the unexplainable bond we seemed to share. "It's complicated," I admitted, looking down at my teacup.

"Complicated," May repeated with a knowing smile, "usually means worth it. If it's love—real love—it'll make you feel more like yourself, not less. Don't run from it because it doesn't fit into a tidy little box."

If Auntie May only knew.

"And don't let fear stop you from embracing it," Effie added, her voice soft but firm. "Sometimes, the things that scare us most are the things we need most."

Oh, yikes! I need a ghost? If they only knew how impossible all this was, but heaven bless them for trying to make me feel better.

I looked between the two women, my heart swelling with gratitude for their words, their laughter, their presence. "You two should host a podcast or something. *Tea and Wisdom with May and Effie.*"

May laughed, looking into her teacup.

Effie's eyes twinkling, she said, "Claire, may you always find your true self, no matter where or with whom."

I smiled, wanting to hug these two, and moved closer to Aunt May. "I will give the spoon thing a try again. First, a hug though."

Aunt May smiled and rose to meet my embrace.

"How long are you here?" I asked Auntie May.

"It's a quick visit. I'm making my rounds to my various properties," May answered. "I'm so happy to see you, dear niece!"

"It's so good to see you too." I returned my aunt's smile.

"I hope you have an unforgettable summer here, Claire, spoon on nose or not." She laughed, looking between Effie and me as we joined in her jubilation.

I found myself nodding as I thought of Angus and how I could certainly never forget him or this castle. Laughter filled the kitchen again, warm and full of life, echoing through the ancient walls like sunlight breaking through the clouds.

The dream began softly as they always did. I found myself in the castle's great hall, though it was not the dim, crumbling space I knew from my waking hours. The tapestries were vibrant, the hearth ablaze, and a warmth infused the air, rich with the scent of lavender and woodsmoke. I turned, and there he was—Angus—standing tall in the firelight, his eyes as deep and endless as the night sky.

"Claire," he said, his voice low and tender, wrapping around me like a beloved melody. He stepped closer, the faintest smile tugging at his lips. "You're here."

"I . . . am," I murmured, my words caught in the tangle of emotions that his presence always stirred. In the dream, the impossibilities of our connection melted away, leaving only the unspoken truths between us.

He reached out, as before, his hand hovering just above mine, as though even in this shared illusion, he feared to break me. But then his fingers brushed mine, solid and warm, and I felt my breath hitch. "I've waited so long," he said, his voice low. "For someone who could see me."

I gazed up at him, my heart heavy with the weight of what could never be. "Angus," I said, my voice trembling suddenly. "Why do you feel so real? Why does this feel so right?"

He smiled then, bittersweet and soft. "Perhaps because it is. Perhaps the universe, in all its strange mercy, has found a way to let us meet across the ages."

The firelight danced in his eyes as he cupped my face, his thumb brushing my cheek. I felt tears prick my eyes, my chest tight with the impossibility of it all.

"But what's the point?" I choked out. "If you're here, and I'm . . . alive, how can this ever be enough?"

He didn't answer. Instead, he drew me closer, his forehead resting against mine. "Don't let go," he whispered. "Not yet."

Angus took my hand gently, his touch impossibly cool, and led me toward the heart of the dreamscape. With a wave of his hand, he took us to the moor, transforming it before my eyes. Silver light deepened into a warm, golden glow, and the stars above rearranged themselves into intricate, shimmering constellations that seemed to pulse in rhythm with my heartbeat.

"Do ye see?" he murmured, his voice reverent. "This is how I see ye, Claire. Ye are my light in the darkness, the beacon I have followed for centuries. Ye have a strength that burns brighter than the sun, a fire that even time cannot dim."

I felt the hotness of tears gathering in my eyes as the constellations cascaded like falling stars, each one swirling around me in luminous trails. They illuminated my hands, my arms, until I could see my entire body glowed.

"Angus," I whispered. "I can't believe this is real. Is it?"

"It is as real as we make it," he replied, his voice thick with emotion.

"This is what lives within ye, lass. This is the light that calls to me."

He stepped closer, his gaze never leaving mine. With another wave of his hand, the stars coalesced into a vision of the castle as it once was, vibrant and whole. I saw people dancing in grand halls, the joy of a world untouched by tragedy.

Time seemed to still as we stood there. The world began fading until there was only him, only his warmth, his voice, his essence. I felt myself falling deeper, losing myself in the moment, my heart breaking even as it soared.

He reached out, his hand brushing my cheek. "Ye are my salvation, Claire. I will fight for ye, always."

The bond I felt with Angus rooted itself more deeply in that moment, became more real than ever before. I could no longer deny the pull that tied me to him.

But as the dream began to blur, the edges of my world dissolved into darkness, and a sharp panic seized me. "Angus!" I cried, gripping his hand as he began to slip away. "Tell me! Please tell me—are you real? Are you truly real?"

His gaze held mine, filled with an aching tenderness that spoke of truths too great for words. "Claire," he said softly, his voice echoing as he began to fade. "You already know the answer."

I awoke with a start, the fading echoes of Angus's voice lingering in my ears like a ghostly melody. I blinked against the dim morning light. My cheeks were damp, my breaths shallow and uneven. It took me a moment to realize that I'd been crying in my sleep.

Wrapping my arms around my knees, I sat up in bed, my heart heavy with a pain that felt as old as the castle walls around me.

"Why?" I whispered into the silence, my voice cracking. The room felt impossibly large, the shadows in the corners pressing in on me like the weight of centuries. The hopelessness was unbearable—he was so close, yet so untouchable, bound by time, by fate, by something I couldn't even name. I pressed my face into my hands, sobbing quietly, not wanting my roommates to hear me.

I felt trapped—trapped between reality and dreams, between what my heart wanted and what the world allowed. Was I losing my mind, clinging to a boy who didn't even belong to my time? Or was this something deeper, a connection that defied logic and reason? I didn't know. All I knew was the ache in my chest, the unbearable wishing for a life I could never have with someone who was already lost to history.

I stayed like that for a long time, my tears soaking into the sleeves of my pajama top, until the cold air of the room began to creep into my skin. Finally, I lay back down, pulling the covers over myself as if they could shield me from the truth. But sleep didn't come. All I could see, even with my eyes closed, was Angus's face vanishing into the mist.

CHAPTER THIRTY-NINE

EXCERPT FROM DIORVAL

Shadows cloaked the room, and the flickering light from
the fireplace cast golden hues on Diorval's face. His eyes,
piercing and smoldering, locked onto mine as if I were
the only thing anchoring him to this existence. I stood
by the window, my arms wrapped around myself, staring
out into the night, the moonlight shining down on me.

Diorval's voice was low, rough with emotion, as he
crossed the room in a few purposeful strides. "I cannot
do this any longer. I cannot stand here watching you live
a life bound by time and death, knowing that with every
passing day, I am losing pieces of you."

I turned to face him, my eyes filled with unshed tears.
"Diorval, you know I can't—"

"You can," he interrupted, his voice fierce now, his
hands trembling as he reached for me. "You think this is
impossible, but look at me! I am proof that eternity exists,
that love can conquer even the unyielding hands of time."

I tried to speak, but no words came. The weight of his
plea held me captive. Yet I was not his long-lost wife. He
had no real feelings for me, only for his delusion about
me. I, on the other hand, had started feeling deeply
for him, even while I loved Ben. I didn't completely

understand it. Somewhere in my heart I was scolding myself for feeling the way I did for both of them.

He continued, his voice softening, "This world—your world—it will take you from me. Slowly, inevitably. One day, you will be gone, and I will be left here, alone again, with nothing but the echo of your laughter and the memory of your touch." His voice cracked, and he dropped his gaze for a moment before looking back at me with an intensity that made my chest tighten.

"But if you come with me, if you choose me, I swear to you, I will make you happier than you ever imagined. Your love will break the curse that keeps me tied to this place—we would be free, together. The world you leave behind will pale in comparison to what we can have. No boundaries. No endings. Just us."

Tears spilled down my cheeks as I stepped toward him, shaking my head even as my heart begged me to surrender. "Diorval, what you're asking is everything. My family, my friends, my life as I know it. How can I—how can I leave it all behind?"

And Ben. I loved him too.

He cupped my face in his hands, his touch as gentle as a whisper, his eyes pleading. "Because I love you. Because some loves are worth leaving everything behind for." His thumb brushed away my tears, and his voice grew quieter, a raw vulnerability slipping through. "Don't make me wait again. Don't make me endure eternity without you. You are my light, my reason. Now that I've found you again, stay with me forever."

The silence stretched between us, thick and charged, until I couldn't hold a sob back any longer. I buried my face in his chest. Diorval held me as if he could shield me from the storm raging inside me, as if the strength of his arms could convince me to choose him.

CHAPTER FORTY

Claire

The studio was oppressively silent, the kind of silence that buzzes in your ears and makes every breath feel like a betrayal. I stood near my finished sculpture, my hands trembling slightly as Professor Stump stormed in, his face red and contorted with fury. The sharp sound of his boots on the stone floor echoed through the room, each step a prelude to the explosion we all knew was coming.

"Who did it?" His voice was a growl, low and menacing, as he slammed a stack of papers onto the nearest table, sending tools and sketches scattering to the floor. "Who had the audacity to file this grievance against me?"

No one moved. No one dared to breathe. My heart pounded in my chest as I exchanged a nervous glance with Joy, who was standing frozen by her own workstation. The professor's eyes were wild, scanning the room like a predator hunting its prey.

"You think you can undermine my authority?" He roared, his voice echoing off the high ceilings. "You think you can question my methods, my standards? Let me make one thing perfectly clear: I am the one who decides your future in this field. Not you. Not some bureaucratic panel!"

He grabbed one of the sculptures—a delicate piece someone had painstakingly worked on and hurled it to the ground. It shattered into pieces, the sound like a gunshot in the tense air. We all flinched. Joy let out a gasp.

"I've reviewed your so-called projects," Stump spat out, his lip curling in disdain. "Mediocre. All of them. Not a single one is worth passing, let alone praising. You should be ashamed to have wasted my time with this garbage." He barked a sudden maniacal laugh, repeating, "Garbage."

A cold wave of anger and fear washed over me. I clenched my fists, my nails biting into my palms, but I said nothing. Confronting him now would only make things worse. Still, the injustice of his words stung like a fresh wound.

Professor Stump's tirade continued, his voice rising and falling in a litany of insults and threats. "Do you think the art world will coddle you like this? Do you think anyone will care about your feelings when your work is torn apart by critics? No! You'll thank me someday for showing you how unworthy you are now!"

He turned abruptly, knocking over another table in his rage. Tools clattered to the floor, some skidding across the room. I saw Effie peek through the cracked door, her face pale with worry, but she didn't enter.

Finally, after what felt like an eternity, Professor Stump stopped, his chest heaving, his face flushed. "I'm failing every single one of you," he hissed, his voice now deadly quiet. "Maybe that will teach you the respect I deserve."

With that, he stormed out, slamming the heavy door behind him. The sound reverberated like a thunderclap, leaving the room in stunned silence. I let out a shaky breath, my body trembling. Around me, the other students stood frozen, their faces pale and eyes wide with fear and disbelief.

Joy stepped closer to me, her voice a whisper. "What do we do now?"

I shook my head, my voice barely audible. "I don't know. But we can't let him get away with this."

For now, though, all we could do was stand in the wreckage of our work, our confidence shattered like the pieces of the sculpture on the floor.

❦

I sat on the edge of my bed, the weight of Stump's abuse pressing down on me like a heavy stone. My phone felt cold in my hands as I waited for the call to connect. It rang once, twice, and then my mom's warm, melodic voice answered.

"Claire, sweetheart! How's my girl?" Mom's voice was like a balm, instantly bringing tears to my eyes.

"M-Mom—" my voice cracked as the dam broke. I pressed my palm to my forehead, trying to keep the sobs at bay. "It's—everything's such a mess.

"Honey, what's wrong? Talk to me," Mom's tone immediately shifted, laced with concern but steadiness, a lifeline I clung to.

I took a shaky breath, my words tumbling out between tears. "It's Professor Stump. He failed me—failed all of us—on our sculpture projects. He's angry because we filed a grievance against him, and he's taking it out on us. Mom, I worked so hard on that piece. I thought I was proud of it, but now I feel like it's all pointless."

"Oh, my love." Mom's voice was soft, soothing. "I am so, so sorry you're going through this. That's so unfair, and it hurts—I can hear it in your voice. But listen to me, Claire. This is not about your talent. This is about his ego, not your work. Do you understand me?"

I sniffled, wiping my tears away with the sleeve of my sweater. "But it feels like maybe I'm not good enough. Maybe he's right."

"No," Mom's voice was firm but kind, the way only a mother's could be. "You are good enough. Claire, you've always been so passionate, so full of creativity and heart. I've seen your work, darling. It's beautiful, just like you. One man's opinion—especially someone as petty as him—doesn't define your worth as an artist or a person."

"But what do I do?" I asked, my voice shaking. "It feels so hopeless right now."

Mom paused for a moment as if carefully choosing her words. "First, you take a deep breath. Then another. And remind yourself that this moment—this pain—isn't permanent. You're strong, Claire, stronger than you think. And you don't have to face this alone. You've got your family, your friends. We're all here for you."

The steadiness of my mom's words made me relax a bit. "I don't want to disappoint you," I whispered.

"Oh, my darling girl, you could never disappoint me. I'm proud of you, not because of your grades or your projects, but because of who you are—talented, kind, brave. You've always faced challenges head-on, and I know you'll get through this too."

I nodded, though Mom couldn't see it. The lump in my throat began to ease. "Thanks, Mom. I really needed to hear that."

"Any time, love. I mean it. And if you need me, you can call, OK? Day or night. And remember, this professor doesn't hold the keys to your future. You do."

"I love you," I said, my voice sounding stronger.

"I love you more," Mom replied warmly. "Now, get some rest, and when you're ready, we'll figure out the next step together. You're not alone, Claire. Not ever."

I hung up, my heart still heavy but now cushioned by my mother's unwavering love. I curled up under my blanket, Mom's words playing over and over in my mind. Slowly, the hopelessness began to fade as a flicker of determination grew.

My stomach growled loudly, reminding me that I should join the others for dinner. A good meal would probably lift my spirits as well. And Effie always made us laugh. I thought of Angus too. I know he would comfort and reassure me. If only he were real.

༄

The pub buzzed with warmth and noise, a sharp contrast to the cold frustration that had gripped the group all day. Dinner had been tasty, bless Effie's heart, but the cloud that hung over us was dark as can be. We remained in a funk, regardless. Later, my friends and I slumped into a corner booth, our faces decidedly stressed. Barry immediately flagged down the bartender, ordering a round of pints and cocktails and ginger ale for the table. The drinks arrived quickly, but the mood remained sour.

"I swear, he lives to make us miserable," Tiffany said, stirring her gin and tonic furiously. Her usually bright face was drawn into a frown. "Failing all of us? How does that even make sense?"

"Power trip," Barry mused darkly. "He's got some kind of god complex. Did you see the smirk on his face? Like he enjoyed it."

"He did enjoy it," Vic added, slamming his beer down on the table. His square jaw was tight with barely restrained rage. "It's not about the work. It's about control. He keeps tearing into us, one by one, but it's been especially bad with Claire."

I shifted uncomfortably, swirling my ginger ale, and muttered. "It's not just about the sculptures. He's got it in for us. And he really hates me."

Joy put a hand on my arm. "And we all know it. But we've got to figure out what we're going to do. We can't just sit here and let him destroy our grades—and our spirits."

"I say we stage a walkout," Carissa suggested, her voice heated. "Refuse to work on anything until the dean steps in."

"Sure,"—Rob snorted, pushing his glasses up his nose—"and get expelled? Sounds like a solid plan."

"Maybe a petition?" Tiffany offered. "That, on top of the grievance we filed, would give it more weight and make it harder for the powers that be to ignore, wouldn't it?"

Julie, who had been unusually quiet until now, leaned forward, her blue eyes glinting mischievously. "Or we could try something a little less conventional."

We all turned to her, curiosity dancing over our faces.

"What do you mean?" I asked.

Julie grinned, pulling her drink closer. "Effie keeps talking about the Ouija board in the common room. What if we . . . I don't know . . . summoned something to teach him a lesson?"

Barry groaned. "Oh, come on, Julie."

"I'm serious!" Julie insisted, raising her hands defensively. "Effie says spirits can help with unresolved anger or injustice. Maybe Lady Red would lend a hand."

I shot her a look. "Effie said to be respectful of the spirits here."

Julie shrugged. "But think about it. Stump's a tyrant. What if we spooked him enough to make him back off?"

"I hate how much I don't hate this idea," Tiffany admitted, her lips curling into a half-smile.

"Julie, I love your chaotic energy, but I don't think summoning ghosts is going to fix this," Barry said with a nervous laugh. "What if we unleash something worse?"

"Worse than Stump?" Vic asked, raising an eyebrow. "I'm not sure that exists."

The table erupted in bitter laughter. For a moment, the tension eased, and our collective frustration melted into solidarity once more.

"OK, fine," Julie conceded, her grin unwavering. "But if he pushes us any further, I'm lighting that candle and calling on the great beyond."

"What are we defining as 'pushing us?'" I asked.

Joy stared a nervous hole through me as Julie answered, "Any more abuse."

I swallowed hard and surveyed the serious expressions around the table.

"I guess we know what's next," Vic said and downed the rest of his beer.

The kitchen was alive with warm smells of vanilla and cinnamon as Joy and I stood side by side at the massive wooden counter, our hands dusted with flour. Effie bustled around us, her energy a blend of cheer and purpose, as she reached for a jar of golden syrup from the shelf.

"I'm just saying,"—Joy huffed, smacking a ball of dough against the counter with perhaps more force than necessary—"if Professor Stump drones on for one more hour about the 'inferior craftsmanship' of every single sculpture we've done, I might start sculpting his likeness just to smash it."

I chuckled, my hands deftly kneading dough. "You'd have to give him his signature scowl. And don't forget the dramatic swoop of his scarf. Do you remember the day he wore a scarf?"

Effie let out a warm laugh as she returned to the counter, her cheeks glowing pink from the heat of the oven. "Och, lassies, don't let that man get under your skin. He thrives on stirring the pot—though I wouldn't trust him to stir one of mine."

Joy snorted, but I felt my smile fading slightly as I brushed a strand of hair from my face. "He's not just stirring the pot, Effie. It's like he's dragging down the whole atmosphere of the castle. Even the sculptures we were working on felt heavier."

Effie paused, a thoughtful expression crossing her face. She placed her hands on the edge of the counter, leaning in closer. "Now, that, my dears, is no small thing. You see, this castle, it breathes. It remembers. And when someone like Professor Stump walks around radiating all that gloom and bile, well, it stirs up more than just the living."

I asked, "You mean the laird and Lady Red?"

Maybe that's why I saw her the other evening, I thought to myself. Stump has disturbed her.

Effie nodded solemnly. "Aye. The laird's a proud spirit, protective of this place. And Lady Red—well, she's got her sorrows, but she's not one to be trifled with. Negativity draws them out like a moth to a flame. I wouldn't be surprised if Professor Stump's rants have set something in motion."

Joy's hands froze mid-roll, her eyes wide. "Wait, are you saying Stump might've angered the ghosts? Like, they're actually active?"

Effie gave a knowing look, her lips curling into a soft smile. "Joy, lass, the spirits here are always active. It's just that most times, they're content to keep their distance. But when someone disturbs the balance . . ." She trailed off, shaking her head. "Well, let's just say it's no coincidence you've both been feeling that heaviness."

I exchanged a glance with Joy, my stomach twisting. "Effie, do you think they're angry? At us?"

Effie reached out and patted my flour-dusted hand. "Not at you, my dear. The laird and the Lady have no quarrel with good-hearted folk. But Stump's energy could unsettle even the calmest of spirits. That's why it's so important for us to counter it."

"And how do we do that?" Joy asked, her voice tinged with both curiosity and apprehension.

Effie's eyes sparkled as she gestured to the dough in our hands. "With this, my lovelies. Baking, laughter, warmth. All of it is a balm for the soul, living or otherwise. You keep bringing light into this place, and I promise you, the spirits will feel it."

The three of us fell into a companionable rhythm, the weight of Stump's negativity gradually giving way to the comforting sounds of rolling pins, bubbling butter, and shared laughter. As the morning stretched on, I couldn't help but feel a little lighter, as though the castle itself was sighing in relief. But part of me held on to some cautionary dread about what Stump may be inviting with his bullying antics.

The sculpture studio was cold, the kind of chill that seemed to seep into my bones no matter how tightly I wrapped the scarf around my neck. Professor Stump prowled the room like a hyena, his long coat sweeping dramatically with every step. He was mid-rant, gesturing wildly at Vic's clay bust with a flourish of disdain.

"This," Stump snarled, pointing a chubby finger at the statue, "is what happens when one lacks vision, discipline, and, dare I say, talent. An amateur's attempt at grandeur. Laughable." Vic's jaw clenched, his hands curling into fists at his sides, but he said nothing. I watched his face, noting the way his cheeks flushed with a mix of embarrassment and fury.

"And you," Stump barked, spinning on Julie, who had been quietly sanding the edges of her clay piece. "Have you even looked at proportions? Or did you think a misshapen blob was an acceptable representation of the human form?"

Julie's hands faltered, her head dropping as she muttered something under her breath.

"What was that?" Stump snapped, stalking toward her. "Speak up! I can't correct what I can't hear, and heaven knows you need correcting."

Julie froze, her knuckles white as she gripped her tools. The room was thick with tension, the oppressive weight of Stump's words pressing down on everyone.

I bit the inside of my cheek as Stump turned toward my table. He loomed over my half-finished sculpture of a woman draped in flowing fabric, his lips curling in mockery.

"Ah, Claire," he drawled, his tone dripping with contempt. "Our resident prodigy. Tell me, is this supposed to be a goddess? A muse? Or is it just another one of your ill-fated attempts at sentimentality?"

"It's meant to convey movement," I said quietly, my heart pounding.

"Movement? *Movement?*" Stump let out a sharp, humorless laugh that echoed around the studio. "This looks more like a sack of laundry left out in the rain. You call this art?"

My face burned, my eyes stinging as I forced myself to keep looking at the sculpture, refusing to give him the satisfaction of meeting his gaze.

"Pathetic," Stump muttered, waving a dismissive hand. "Do better or stop wasting my time."

The silence that followed was deafening, broken only by the soft clatter of Julie's tools as she set them down. Vic shot me a sympathetic glance, his jaw still tight. Julie looked at him, then at me, her eyes narrowing in a way that made my stomach twist. The others, too, exchanged glances—dark, calculating, and eerily calm.

As the class ended and Stump swept out of the room in a whirl of fabric and disdain, I gathered my things, my movements noticeably shaky. The atmosphere in the studio was thick with an unspoken energy, and I caught snatches of whispered conversations between Vic and Julie.

"It's gone too far," Vic muttered.

"We'll fix it," Julie said, her voice steady but low. "The first full moon we get."

My heart sank. I didn't need to ask what they were talking about. The Ouija board. Effie's warnings echoed in my mind, but I could already see the determination on their faces. I wondered what Angus would have to say about it. I swallowed hard, my throat tight as a terrible thought took hold. *What if they do it? What if they summon something we can't control?*

I didn't have an answer, but the uneasy prickle at the back of my neck told me I'd soon find out.

Another dream. I stood in the castle's great hall, its stone walls flickering with the soft glow of torchlight. The air was warmer than I remembered, filled with the faint scent of heather and something richer, deeper, that I could only describe as *him*. Angus stood at the far end of the hall, leaning casually against the grand hearth, his dark eyes fixed on me with that familiar intensity that sent my pulse racing.

"Claire," he said softly, his voice carrying over the crackling fire as if it were a whisper meant only for me. He pushed off the hearth and strode toward me. But there was something in his expression tonight—a shadow of hesitation.

"Angus, you're here," I breathed.

"Aye," he said, his lips curving into a faint smile that didn't quite reach his eyes. "I cannae stay away."

He reached out, his hand hovering near mine but not quite touching. The space between us felt electric, charged with words left unsaid. I wanted to step closer, to close the gap, but something in his posture held me back.

"I've been searching," he said, his voice low and rough, "for a way to bridge this divide between us. It's no small task, breaking the laws of the living and the dead."

My breath caught up. "You think it's possible?"

Angus's jaw tightened, and he looked away for a moment, his gaze sweeping over the hall as though the ancient stones might hold the answer. "I dinnae," he admitted, his voice little more than a whisper. "But I'll not rest until I've tried every path."

His eyes found mine again, dark with despair. "Do ye not see, Claire? Ye've awakened something in me that I've never known before. I willna let it slip away."

My chest tightened, and I dared to step closer, the hem of my dress brushing against him. "Angus, I don't want to lose you. But this isn't fair to either of us."

He raised a hand, brushing his knuckles against my cheek. The sensation was strange, like the warmth of sunlight through a cold window—real, yet not quite tangible. "I'll find a way," he murmured, his voice fierce. "For us."

The words wrapped around me like a promise, pulling me deeper into the dream. But then his expression shifted, darkening with a sudden urgency. His hand dropped, and he stepped back, his gaze sharpening as though he were thinking of something dreadful.

"Claire," he said, his tone grave, "ye must be wary. Yer friends, yer cohort—they're playing wi' fire, dabbling in forces they dinnae understand."

I blinked, my heart thudding. "You mean the Ouija board?"

"Aye," he said, his voice heavy with warning. "The veil between this world and theirs is thin here, thinner than most. If they open that veil, they'll find the wrong kind of attention. Spirits that dinnae share my goodwill."

With a wave of his hand, he showed me the familiar scene of people dancing and celebrating in the great hall of the castle, carefree and vibrant with life. Then, just as quickly, the vision shattered into darkness.

the joyous laughter replaced by mournful wails. Shadows crept along the walls, and the castle stood in ruin.

"That," Angus said, his voice breaking, "is what happens when the spirits are disrupted. And yet, when I look at ye, I dare to hope."

My heart skipped as I stared at him, his vulnerability unraveling every defense I had. "Angus, what should I do?" I asked, fear rising in my voice.

"If they persist,"—his form began to blur at the edges, as though the dream were unraveling—"be ready."

"Ready for what?" I cried, stepping toward him as he faded, my fingers grasping at nothing.

His final words echoed through the empty hall as I woke with a start, my heart racing wildly.

"For the price they might pay."

CHAPTER FORTY-ONE

Kaya

The moon hung high in the midnight sky, casting a cold, silver glow over Kaya's restless figure. She tossed and turned, her sheets tangled around her legs as the nightmare ensued.

Kaya stood in the shadow of the castle, its towering stone walls looming ominously against the darkened sky. The air was heavy and the once-majestic building seemed alive with an ancient, unseen energy. Somewhere in the distance, thunder rumbled, though no rain fell.

"Claire!" Kaya called, her voice echoing against the walls. It was swallowed almost immediately by the oppressive silence that followed. She began to climb the worn steps leading to the castle door, her heart pounding with an unshakable sense of urgency. The massive oak door creaked open of its own accord, revealing a long corridor lit by flickering torches.

At the far end of the hallway, Kaya saw her daughter. Claire was sitting on the cold, stone floor, her back turned to her mother. A faint red glow surrounded her, and Kaya's chest tightened as she noticed the faint outline of a figure—a young woman—standing just behind Claire, her flowing red dress shimmering like fire in the dim light.

"Claire!" Kaya shouted again, this time her voice trembling with fear. She tried to run toward her, but her feet felt like they were sinking into the floor, the stones grasping at her like quicksand.

Claire didn't turn, didn't respond. Instead, her head tilted slightly, as though she were listening intently to the shadowy figure looming over her.

"Leave her alone!" Kaya screamed, desperation lacing her voice. "Claire, get up! Come to me!"

The figure slowly turned its head, and Kaya froze. The young woman's face was obscured, her features twisted and blurred, but her eyes—two glowing embers—pierced through the darkness, looking upon Kaya with an unnatural intensity. A young lady, glowing red.

"Too late," the young lady said, her voice a chilling whisper that seemed to come from everywhere at once. "She belongs to the castle now."

"No!" Kaya cried, finally breaking free of the floor's grip. She lunged forward, but the young woman raised a hand, and a wall of invisible force slammed into Kaya, knocking her backward. She hit the ground hard, the air rushing from her lungs.

When she looked up again, Claire was gone. The torches extinguished one by one, plunging the corridor into complete darkness. Kaya's heart raced as she scrambled to her feet, the walls seeming to close in on her.

"Claire!" she sobbed, her voice echoing into the void. The silence that followed was deafening.

Then, a whisper, faint but clear, brushed against her ear: "She can't leave, Kaya."

The ground beneath her crumbled, and Kaya felt herself falling into an endless abyss, the young woman's laughter echoing around her as she plunged into the darkness.

Kaya woke with a start, her breath ragged, her body drenched in sweat. The room was still, but the echo of the young woman's words lingered in her ears. She clutched her chest, her heart pounding as she whispered, "Claire, what have I done, letting you stay there?"

Cole snored softly beside her. She was glad she hadn't woken him this time.

The moonlight streaming through the window seemed cold somehow as Kaya sat up in bed. She was unable to shake the feeling that, somehow, the castle was watching.

CHAPTER FORTY-TWO

Claire

The phone buzzed against my cheek as I sat curled up in a plush armchair by the crackling fire in the common room. My mother's voice on the other end was shaken.

"I had a dream, Claire," Mom said, her voice noticeably sounding worried. "You were in the castle, and something wasn't right."

I sighed, leaning my head back against the chair. "Mom, I'm fine. I promise. It's just an old castle with a lot of history—and OK, maybe a few cracks and drafts—but nothing is going to happen to me."

I should've known that my mother would feel my worry, my dread. She was so intuitive—so in tune with Gini and me. She always had been. But I couldn't let her worry. My sense of things was shifting ever so slightly. I had to accept that fate was somehow writing itself. I grappled with my limited influence on all of it. I could share my concerns and my worries, but if no one listened to me, I had to carry on and let everything unravel on its own accord. Still, it was very difficult to let go at times. But something was telling me I had to.

Mom's voice softened, but her concern was still palpable. "I know you're brave, Claire. But that place is different. I can feel it. Please be careful."

"I will, Mom," I said gently, trying to soothe her. "And you know Auntie May is always a text away. Plus, Effie would probably set up a shrine to ward off bad vibes if anything even remotely spooky happened."

I prayed I was right.

Mom let out a faint chuckle, though the tension didn't leave her voice entirely. "All right, sweetheart. Just don't ignore your instincts. And call me if you need anything."

"I will. Love you."

"Love you too, Claire."

The call ended, and I set my phone aside, gazing into the fire for a moment before heading up to my room. Mom was very sensitive. It was an amazing gift she had that she could tap into my feelings, and more than that, tap into the broader circumstances. There's no way I could tell her everything—she'd never sleep. The day had been long, and sleep came fast.

The dream took me down a long, winding corridor, the stone walls dimly lit by flickering torchlight. But I wasn't alone. Lady Red stood at the far end of the hall, her crimson gown looking as though it were made of liquid fire.

"Come," the lady said, her voice smooth and commanding. "There is something you must see."

Though my instincts screamed to turn away, my feet moved of their own accord. I followed Lady Red as she glided through the halls, her movements unnaturally graceful. They passed rooms I recognized and others I didn't, descending a spiral staircase that seemed to plunge deeper than the castle's foundations.

Finally, we stopped at a small alcove carved into the stone. It was almost hidden, tucked behind a faded tapestry depicting a hunt. The lady turned to me, her expression unreadable. "It waits for you here."

I hesitated, my hand trembling as I reached out to pull back the tapestry. Behind it, I saw a narrow shelf built into the wall, and resting there was an old, leather-bound journal, its cover cracked with age.

"What is it?" I whispered.

Lady Red's lips curved into a faint, enigmatic smile. "The truth."

My eyes snapped open, my heart racing as I stared at the rafters above me. The dream had felt so vivid, so real, like the ones with Angus always felt. I sat up, the memory of the alcove burning in my mind.

The moment I opened my eyes the next morning, curiosity and unease propelled me through the castle's winding corridors. Honestly, I felt a little crazy while retracing the dream's path the best I could, my steps echoing in the quiet. When I reached the spot from my dream, I stopped short, my breath catching in my throat.

'What are the odds?' I thought.

The faded tapestry hung just as it had in my dream. With trembling hands, I pulled it back—and there it was.

The alcove.

The shelf.

The journal.

My fingers brushed over the cracked leather as I lifted the journal from its resting place. I shivered, unable to deny the weight of the moment. The journal felt heavy with secrets, as though the very castle had been waiting for me to find it.

As I opened it, the faint scent of aged paper filled the air. On the first page, written in spidery handwriting, were the words:

To those who seek the truth, tread carefully. The past holds more than answers——it holds power.

My hands tightened on the book, and for a moment, I felt as though I were being watched. I rushed back to my room, eager and nervous to read whatever was inside.

I waited until the room was empty and everyone was gone for breakfast.

The journal's pages were fragile, the edges curling and yellowed with time. I sat cross-legged on the cold, stone floor of my room. Sitting on the floor gave me the grounded, solid feeling I needed while venturing into the unknown world these pages held. My fingers brushed over the spidery handwriting, and the words seemed to possess an eerie vitality, as though the emotions behind them had refused to fade over the centuries.

> *To whoever finds this record: know that my tale is one of love, betrayal, and ruin. My name will be lost in time, but I was known for my fiery red tresses, and my story is etched into the bones of the castle.*

The handwriting was uneven, the ink smudged in places as though written in haste—or grief. I leaned closer, my heart racing as I read on. This was Lady Red's journal—I felt that deep inside my heart.

> *He was my laird, my protector, and my undoing. With his dark eyes and his sharper wit, he was young, but he ruled the castle not just with strength but with a heart too large for the burdens placed upon it. Against all reason, I loved him, though I was bound to another——a match made for alliance, not for love.*

My breath hitched. The journal seemed to thrum with the weight of those words, as though Lady Red's love still echoed through the stone walls of the castle.

We thought ourselves clever, stealing moments in the shadows, our love burning brighter with each secret embrace. But secrets in a castle such as this are as fleeting as mist. We were discovered by my husband, no less. His wrath was swift, his betrayal deeper than the blade he drove into my lover's side.

My hands tightened on the journal. I could almost see it: the blood on the laird's hands, Lady Red's scream echoing in the cold stone corridors.

I sought vengeance, blinded by grief and guilt. I turned to the seer who lived in the woods beyond the castle, her eyes clouded with wisdom and sorrow. I begged her to bring him back, to give us a second chance. But love surrounded by deceit is a dangerous thing, and the ritual she offered me required a sacrifice greater than my heart could bear.

The next lines were smeared, but I could make out fragments:

a binding of blood,
. . . souls tethered,
. . . vengeance given life.

*The ritual went wrong. My lover did not
return to me——not as he was. Instead, his spirit
became tied to this place, a shadow of his former self,
bound by the betrayal that ended his life. And I
was cursed to remain in the castle, too, my sorrow
intended to feed the walls, my love turned to ash.
Together, we remain unable to move forward, unable
to forgive.*

My eyes burned as I turned the page. The writing grew more erratic, as though Lady Red's desperation had bled into the ink.

*The curse binds us both, our unresolved pain
forever known to anyone who disturbs the castle's
balance——anyone who brings conflict and cruelty.
As my fallen lover showed me, the veil grows
thin here, and the castle hungers for souls in search
of love.*

The final lines were written in a jagged script, almost scratched.

*If there is a way to break the curse, it lies in love
stronger than death and truth braver than fear.
But tread carefully, for the past does not let go
easily, and the cost of freedom may be a price too
great.*

I closed the journal, my hands trembling. My mind spun with images of Lady Red and her lover, their forbidden love twisted into something monstrous by betrayal and grief. I could feel the weight of the curse pressing down on the castle, on me.

As I sat there, the faintest whisper brushed against my ear, a young woman's voice, haunting yet familiar: "Do you see now, Claire? Do you see what binds us?"

The room felt colder, the air heavier. I didn't understand how I could be part of the curse—how was I part of a forbidden love gone wrong?

Unless . . .

Angus.

Why had he not introduced himself as the laird? Didn't he say that he'd not known love before? My stomach turned.

I clutched the journal tighter, my resolve hardening. Lady Red was calling on me to break the curse—but I couldn't fathom how that would be possible.

CHAPTER FORTY-THREE

Claire

P athetic," Professor Stump sneered, stopping in front of Vic's sculpture. It was a striking piece—a rough-hewn figure of a man mid-struggle, as if emerging from the stone itself—but Stump saw only flaws. "This isn't art. This is an embarrassment. Did you even consider proportion? Balance? Or did you just start hacking away and hope for the best?"

The air in the studio was heavy as wet clay, thick with the silence of a group too drained to protest. Professor Stump paced before us, his hands clasped behind his back like some self-appointed arbiter of artistic worth. The click of his boots on the stone floor echoed in the cavernous room, each step a punctuation to his scathing words.

Vic's knuckles whitened as he gripped the edge of his worktable, his lips pressed into a thin line. The rest of the cohort watched in tense silence, our collective anger simmering just beneath the surface. Julie glanced at me, her expression tight. A silent knowing passed between us.

Stump turned abruptly, his sharp eyes landing on Julie's clay bust. He snatched it off the table without asking, turning it in his hands as though searching for every possible imperfection. "And this. Is this what you call craftsmanship? Look at these features—crude, lifeless, amateurish. Do you even care about what you're creating?"

Julie's face flushed with obvious embarrassment and anger, but she said nothing. I could see the restraint in her clenched jaw, the way her hands trembled ever so slightly as she fought to keep her composure.

Then, Stump's gaze landed on my work, a delicate figure of a woman, her form draped in flowing fabric, the folds of which I had painstakingly carved to suggest movement and grace. He scoffed as he approached, tilting his head like a bird of prey about to strike.

"Ah, Claire," he drawled. "Our little genius. Tell me, do you think sentimentality will save this mess? It's sloppy. Predictable. A child's notion of elegance. If you spent half as much time studying technique as you do indulging in your fanciful whims, you might produce something of worth."

My face burned with a mix of humiliation and fury. I opened my mouth to respond, but the weight of the cohort's silent anger stopped me. They had their plan. Enduring Stump's tirade was just the fuel they needed to justify what was coming.

"Enough," Stump barked, setting the sculpture down carelessly, his dismissive tone cutting through the room. "Clearly, some of you haven't learned a thing. Consider this your wake-up call: art is not about your feelings or your fragile egos. It's about excellence, and frankly, I don't see much of that here."

The cohort remained silent, their expressions hard and unyielding as Stump turned on his heel and stormed out. The door slammed, and for a moment, the only sound was the faint hum of the overhead lights.

Julie was the first to break the silence, muttering under her breath, "He'll get what's coming to him."

The others nodded, and I could feel the seething anger emanating from their collective. Vic set his jaw, glancing at me.

I couldn't shake the gnawing dread in my stomach. I had heard them plotting more details of how they would summon something or someone to teach Stump a lesson he'd never forget. I had warned them yet again about the dangers of upsetting the spirits, the dangers of manipulating them. They weren't to be toyed with, but my classmates were not ready to listen.

As they exchanged dark glances, a sudden, sharp clang startled everyone. We turned to see a paint jar tumbling off a shelf, its lid popping open. As it hit the ground, bright red paint spilled out, pooling like blood across the floor.

The room grew colder, and I swore I felt the faintest touch brush across my shoulder. We stared at the spill, stunned in silence.

Julie swallowed hard, her voice a whisper. "Was that—?"

Before she could finish, an unmistakable chill moved through the studio, sending shivers down my spine.

Lady Red was watching.

I stormed out of the sculpture studio, my bag slung haphazardly over my shoulder as I nearly collided with Vic and Joy loitering by the castle's narrow stone corridor. Vic was mid-laugh, boot propped up against the wall, while Joy stood nervously twisting her hair between her fingers.

"There you are!" My eyes darted around for any eavesdropping classmates, and I lowered my voice. "Are you serious about the Ouija board?"

Vic grinned, seemingly unbothered by my urgency. "It's not just a Ouija board, Claire. It's justice. Professor Stump needs a little reminder that he's not the only one who can make life miserable. Besides, everyone's in on it."

I turned to Joy, who looked decidedly less enthusiastic. "Joy, come on. You can't really think this a good idea."

Joy gave a small shrug. "It's not that I think it's a good idea. It's just—well, what's the harm? It's will probably just be a bunch of us sitting around, drinking, and waiting for nothing to happen."

I sighed, exasperated. "The harm is that you're messing with things you don't understand. Haven't you both heard the stories? Effie's been warning us since day one. People have tried stuff like this here before and—"

"And what?" Vic interrupted, leaning forward with mock curiosity. "The ghosts come out and pull someone's hair? Boo-hoo. Sounds better than another two-hour lecture from Stump about 'texture' and 'visual harmony.'"

I resisted the urge to strangle him. "You don't know what you're inviting in! Vic, it's not funny. I've been dreaming about—"

I stopped short, biting my lip. The last thing I needed was to bring up Angus and get labeled the castle lunatic.

Joy looked at me with knowing eyes.

"Never mind. Look, this is dangerous. What if something does happen? What if you summon something that doesn't want to leave us alone?"

Vic rolled his eyes and pushed off the wall, standing to his full, gangly height. "Claire, you're overreacting. It's a board game. Parker Brothers didn't exactly craft these things to summon demons. We're just gonna send Professor Stump a warning, a message from beyond. You know, scare him a little. He deserves that much."

"Deserving it doesn't mean it's a good idea," I shot back, my voice sharp. "Joy?"

Joy hesitated, glancing between Vic and me. "I mean, if it starts feeling weird, I'll leave. OK?"

I groaned. "Unbelievable." Looking Vic in the eye, I added, "Don't say I didn't warn you when you wake up at 3:00 a.m. with something breathing down your neck."

Vic smirked, utterly unshaken. "If it means that Stump fears his own shadow the rest of this term, it'll be worth it."

I watched him saunter down the hall without a care in the world. I turned back to Joy, who gave me a pat on my arm. "I'll keep an eye on him. I promise," Joy murmured.

"I don't think that will be enough," I replied in a low voice. "I'm scared for all of us."

The full moon would be here any day now. The dread inside me grew ever stronger. They were going to follow through. Nothing could sway them from their plan.

CHAPTER FORTY-FOUR

EXCERPT FROM DIORVAL

I stood frozen in the grand hall, the air around me humming with an unnatural energy. The veil shimmered before me, a translucent barrier of silvery light that emanated energy like a living thing. Beyond it, the world looked like a dream: lush fields of golden grass rippling under an endless twilight, ancient trees with branches that seemed to hum with music, and a sky dusted with stars that blinked in patterns I almost recognized.

Diorval's voice cut through the enchantment, smooth and coaxing. "You don't belong here, my love. You never have. This world has always been too small for you, its people too blind to see what you truly are."

He stepped closer, his dark robes swirling as though stirred by an unseen wind. His eyes, glowing faintly, locked onto mine with an intensity that made my heart pound. "Here. beyond the veil, you will find your true self. Power. Purpose. Freedom from their petty concerns and judgment. You can finally leave pain behind, and we can be together again. Forever."

My breath was caught up. Having tried to convince him I was not his long-lost wife had failed on every attempt. He was convinced I had lost my true identity while traversing the veil. I took a step forward, an unconscious movement on my behalf. The warmth radiating from the veil was intoxicating, mesmerizing, as it pulled me toward it with an almost physical force. I felt the weight of expectations from the world melting away. Diorval was right—hadn't I always felt awkward and out of place?

"You're hesitating," he said, his voice laced with something like pity. "Why? For them? The ones who don't appreciate you? They never will. But I see you. The real you."

His words wrapped around me like a spell, and I felt myself reach for the veil, brushing its surface. Cool and soft, like water but not wet, as it touched my skin. A gasp escaped me as a sensation flooded my senses. It felt like being filled with light, so gentle and warm. It made me long for more of its life force.

"Just one step," Diorval urged in a whisper that seemed to echo through me. "One step, and you'll be free."

I looked back over my shoulder. The castle's familiar stone walls were suddenly cold and uninviting. Behind me were the voices of my world—my mother and father's encouragement and laughter, Ben's loving gaze. They were distant now, like a song fading into silence. Yet they tethered me, a fragile thread pulling me away from the shimmering promise in front of me.

My chest tightened as I stepped closer to the veil, the light bathing everything in its ethereal glow. I stood on the threshold, my hand trembling in midair, caught between two worlds.

"Emily, choose," he said firmly, commanding me. "You cannot linger forever."

Tears pricked my eyes as my heart warred with itself. I took a shaky breath, my gaze fixed on the mesmerizing world beyond the veil. Yet, even as it called to me, the echoes of my old life refused to let go. I stood there, poised at the edge, unable to decide.

CHAPTER FORTY-FIVE

Claire

My dreamscape blurred and shifted, and the familiar castle walls melted away into an endless moor bathed in an eerie silver light. Argus stood before me, his expression more open, more raw than I had ever seen. His usual confidence faltered, and a tremor in his voice demonstrated his vulnerability.

"Claire," he began, his voice low and rough with emotion, "I can no longer pretend time is on our side. There is a curse that holds me here, and ye are the only one who can break it, lass. I . . . I dinna how to ask this of ye, but there is no one else."

My heart ached at the sight of him, so strong yet so clearly burdened. "Why me, Angus?" I whispered. "Why am I the one who has to fix this?" But I knew the answer deep inside. After finding the journal, I felt assured about what I needed to do.

"Because ye are the one I have waited for," he confessed, stepping closer. His eyes, filled with a mix of longing and despair, held me captive. "For centuries, I've dreamed of ye. Ye are the only soul who can see me—truly see me. Ye have the strength, the light, that no one else possesses. But,"—he hesitated, his gaze dropping—"I fear I am selfish. I should want ye to be free, to live yer life without this burden. Yet I find myself unable to let ye go. My feelings for ye . . . they are real, Claire. They have always been real."

My breath caught in my throat. His words pulled at my heart, but a shadow of doubt crept in. "Angus, if this curse is as dangerous as you say, how can I trust that you're telling me everything? How can I know that you're not keeping something from me?"

Angus looked as though I had struck him. "I would never lie to ye, lass. But I am haunted by my own guilt, my own failures. It was my recklessness that brought this curse upon the castle, upon my people. I canna forgive myself, and yet . . . I . . . I canna stop loving ye."

The moor seemed to grow colder as the weight of his confession settled between us. I wrapped my arms around myself, torn between the deep connection I felt with Angus and the fear of what breaking the curse might mean for my own life.

"Claire," he said softly, stepping even closer, "I canna ask ye to sacrifice everything for me. But know this: Whatever ye choose, my heart will always be yours."

I stood on the threshold of decision, the silver light of the dreamscape casting an otherworldly glow. My heart waged a battle deep within as I stared at him, his vulnerability unraveling my resolve. Was he my destiny or my undoing? The answer remained just out of reach, lost in the shadows of the dream as I awoke.

I found my cohort gathered in the castle's dimly lit drawing room, where candles flickered ominously around the Ouija board. Joy had let me know that Julie decided to begin this venture ahead of the full moon, which was her original plan.

Laughter and nerves filled the room as Vic placed his hands confidently on the planchette. "Let's see what secrets this old place is hiding," he said, grinning, a mischievous glint in his eyes.

I felt helpless and disappointed as I stood near the door, taking in the whole scene. They didn't care to listen to my warnings. Fed up and fueled by anger, they wanted revenge on Professor Stump at any cost.

The moment they began, the atmosphere shifted. The room grew colder, the air suffocating and oppressive. The planchette moved with frightening speed, spelling out messages none of them could understand. A vase toppled from a nearby table, shattering against the stone floor. Julie shrieked as the shadows in the corners stretched toward them.

I shivered as I felt the air begin to feel charged. Absentmindedly, I fiddled with my bracelet.

Suddenly, Effie burst through the door, her face pale and voice trembling. "Stop this! You have no idea what you're tampering with!"

Vic, emboldened by the strange activity, pressed on. "One more question," he said, ignoring the rising tension. "Who are we speaking to?"

The planchette froze for a moment before moving violently. The candles flickered before going out, plunging the room into darkness. A piercing scream rang out and echoed through the halls, not from any of the students but from somewhere deep within the castle.

Emerging from the shadows, a chilling figure draped in a blood-red gown radiated both beauty and terror.

Lady Red.

Her voice was like a mournful wind as she cried, "Fools! You meddle in what you do not understand. The curse binds us all, and your arrogance will awaken what should remain in slumber."

As my classmates cowered in terror, Lady Red's fiery gaze settled on me. "You, girl," she said, her voice laced with both warning and sorrow. "The fate of all rests on your shoulders. Stop them before it is too late, or you will all pay the price."

With that, Lady Red vanished, leaving the room in an icy silence. I stood frozen, the weight of the spirit's words pressing heavily on me. My classmates looked toward me, their faces pale and fearful. The castle itself seemed to groan in the aftermath, its ancient walls bearing witness to the calamity they had unleashed.

"Will you stop now?" I yelled, tears threatening to erupt from my eyes.

I looked between Vic and Julie, and though they appeared adequately frightened, neither one assured me that they were done with what they'd started. The stony expressions of resignation on the other's faces augmented what I feared most. And then, the night pressed down on me as I decided what I needed to do.

"I need the truth, Angus," I began, confronting him in the stillness of my dream. We stood inches apart in the great hall, illuminated by only moonlight. My voice was firm despite the tumult in my chest. "All of it. What aren't you telling me?"

He hesitated, the anguish in his eyes deepening. "Ye dinna want to hear this, lass."

"I have to," I insisted. "If I'm to break this curse, I need to know everything."

Angus sighed, his shoulders slumping under the weight of centuries. "The curse . . . it was nae just born of tragedy. It was born of betrayal. My betrayal."

My breath remained in my chest as I stayed silent, urging him to continue.

"There was another," he began, his voice cracking. "Lady Red. She is more than a ghost, Claire. She was the girl I loved. But our love—it was forbidden. I became the laird when I was young—stupid and inexperienced. When the castle came under attack, I made a choice. I sacrificed the lives of the innocent, some of them her people, some mine, and the soldiers who trusted me. All to protect her, to protect us."

He turned away, his jaw clenched. "But it was a selfish love, and it came at a cost. The people I betrayed and their pain, their deaths bound themselves to the castle. Lady Red—her anger, her sorrow, it feeds the curse. And my guilt binds me here, as surely as her grief holds her spirit in torment."

I tried to speak, but my voice remained a whisper. "You betrayed them for her?"

"Aye," Angus admitted, his voice trembling. "And I have lived with that guilt every moment since. Her love turned to rage when she found out what I had done. Now, she is the heart of the curse, her anguish an unending storm that keeps us all bound."

I felt my world tilt, the weight of his confession crashing over me. "So, this isn't just about freeing you. It's about stopping her so they all can be free."

Angus nodded, his eyes dark with regret. "I dinna ask for forgiveness, Claire. I dinna deserve it. But ye have the strength to end this. To bring peace to the castle, to Lady Red, and to me. Only the purity of an unselfish love can end all this misery. Even if you decide to hate me later for everything I've done."

Tears streamed down my face as I struggled to process his words. The boy I had grown to care for was both the victim and villain, bound by love and guilt in equal measure. "I don't hate you," I said finally, my voice weak. "But I don't know if I can do this."

"Ye can. It's why you're here. There are no accidents, Claire," Angus said, stepping closer. His voice was filled with quiet conviction. "Ye must break the curse."

CHAPTER FORTY-SIX

Claire

I tossed and turned beneath the weight of my tangled thoughts. The echoes of Angus's confession played endlessly in my mind, each word laced with sorrow and a love that both frightened and enchanted me. My dreams offered no solace, only shadows of Lady Red's furious eyes and the cries of those Angus had betrayed. By the time dawn broke, my body felt as heavy as my spirit.

I wandered through the castle's labyrinthine halls the next morning, hoping to find my cohort and talk some sense into them. The silence was unnerving, the usual chatter and footsteps conspicuously absent. By midday, it dawned on me that they were likely at the pub, huddled together, no doubt, planning their Ouija board ritual for tonight. Anxiety twisted my gut as I imagined what their carelessness might unleash.

At lunch, I sat with Effie in the sunlit kitchen. Effie's usual warmth was tinged with a worried edge. "Ye look pale, lass," Effie said, her sharp eyes narrowing as she pushed a hearty soup bowl toward me.

I forced a smile. "It's been a lot, and I'm tired."

Effie nodded knowingly. "Aye, I feel it too. The castle's restless. Something's stirring, and it's nae just yer classmates' foolishness."

I hesitated, my spoon hovering over the bowl. "Do you think they will make things worse tonight?"

Effie leaned forward, her voice dropping to a whisper. "Worse? Lass, ye it will. Spirits dinna take kindly to meddling, and this castle's seen its share of pain. If they awaken somethin' they cannae control, it'll be on yer shoulders to stop it. Ye have a connection they dinna understand. Remember that."

I nodded, my appetite vanishing. I tried to reassure myself, but the knot in my stomach only tightened as the day wore on. I spent the rest of the day in the studio, trying to clear my mind and ease my worries, but the sun's descent marked the approach of a turbulent night.

As the ancient clock chimed, echoing through the halls, I searched the castle. It was nearing midnight. I dreaded what might happen with my classmates using the Ouija board. I found my cohort huddled in the turret, their faces illuminated by the wavering light of several candles. The Ouija board was already set, its planchette trembling under eager fingers.

"Claire!" Vic said with a grin, his bravado masking the nervous energy that filled the room. "You're just in time. We're asking the spirits for a little poetic justice—Professor Stump is long overdue for a lesson of his own."

"Stop this," I said firmly, my voice cutting through the murmurs. "You have no idea what you're doing."

But the group ignored me, their attention focused on the board as it began to move. The air temperature plummeted. The planchette spelled out a single word: Justice.

Once again, the candles snuffed out in unison, taking the room into total darkness. A low, mournful wail echoed through the turret, followed by the sound of something heavy scraping across the stone floor. Shadows danced wildly, forming shapes that seemed to stretch toward us.

Then she appeared.

Lady Red manifested in full, her crimson gown swirling as if caught in an unseen tempest. Her fury was palpable, her voice a chilling mixture of sorrow and rage. "You dare disturb the balance? Fools! You meddle in matters beyond your comprehension. Leave this place or suffer the consequences."

This time, the screams of my cohort filled the room as they ran out the door in a flurry, the room erupting into chaos. The Ouija board flew across the space, crashing against the wall before igniting as it hit the floor. A wind whipped through the turret, though the solitary window remained closed.

"Angus!" I shouted, my voice cracked as I urged him. "Help me!"

Angus appeared beside me with a grim expression. He grabbed my hand and squeezed tightly. I felt my entire body begin to radiate intense heat as together we projected a light that emitted a calmness over the entire space. It was as though our bond acted as an anchor against the storm. I stepped forward, my voice steady despite the fear clawing at my chest. "Please! We didn't mean to harm you! Let us fix all that has been wrong!"

Lady Red's gaze locked onto mine. "You would risk your soul for them? For him? Foolish girl. You walk the path of ruin."

The air shifted and I felt an icy grip on my heart. My knees buckled, but Angus caught me. "Claire, stop!"

"I can't let this go on!" I cried. "Do not harm them! Let everyone go free! Everyone!" I demanded, shaking inside. "Angus too!"

Lady Red's rage intensified, her eyes glowing hot like embers. I could see the torment building inside of Angus. His expression was ragged, torn, his ethereal form weakening.

"Lady Red!" he called, his voice resonating with a supernatural force. "Yer quarrel is with me. Release her and take what ye need from me instead!"

Lady Red hesitated, her spectral form flickering. "You would give yourself over? Even knowing you will be lost forever?"

"Aye," Angus replied, his voice breaking. "If it means sparin' her, I would. Let her go!"

"No!" I cried, clutching at him. "You can't do this!"

Angus turned to me, his expression soft. "Claire, this is my choice. My penance. Yer heart is true. Ye've given me hope, but ye deserve to live free of this place, of me."

The Lady Red's anger wavered, her form dimming. "The curse demands resolution! But perhaps—perhaps, there is another way."

She reached toward me, her cold hand grabbing my wrist. "If you take his place, the curse will end. But your life as you know it will be over."

My heart pounded, the weight of the choice crushing me. I looked at Angus, tears streaming down my face. "There has to be another way!"

But Angus shook his head. "There isnae time. Claire, live for me." He stepped between Lady Red and me, offering himself.

Lady Red's face twisted into a satisfied grin as she released me and extended her hand toward Angus, her spectral grip tightening. As his form began fading, his gaze never left me. His light slowly dimmed. "I love ye, Claire. Always," he whispered

I sobbed, grasping for him. "Angus! No, don't go! I love you!"

The room flashed in a blinding light. I hid my face from the blaze, and when I opened my eyes, Angus had vanished.

I stared in disbelief, shaken at the thought of where Angus had gone.

In the following moment, the walls began expanding and warping as a low, mournful wail filled the room, growing into a howling chorus of voices—centuries of rage and sorrow unleashed at last. The air itself trembled as ghostly figures flickered into existence, their forms shifting between transparency and solidity, their eyes burning with the light of vengeance. Shadows writhed and moaned, seeming to come from the stones themselves.

The room was changing, melting away from the familiar into something unrecognizable. The floor beneath me rippled like water, and I stumbled as a sinking feeling overtook me. The walls twisted again, bending in impossible ways and stretching into a labyrinth as more shadows gathered, funneling around Lady Red. Swirling and hissing, the shadows spiked in the tornado they created.

I couldn't breathe, couldn't think.

Lady Red staggered back, her crimson gown flowing like blood in the moonlight. "No! You belong to me!" she shrieked, her voice raw with anger. "You are bound by my will!"

But the spirits no longer cowered. They surged forward, spectral hands stretching toward her, their touch turning her skin a ghastly gray. She screamed, a sound that rattled the very bones of the castle, but there was no escape. Then, the shadows began whirling so fast, engulfing Lady Red until I could barely see her.

The spirits swirled around her, lifting her from the ground. Her body convulsed as their icy grasp seeped into her, pulling, tearing— unraveling the dark magic that had bound them for so long. Flames erupted from her skin, licking up her arms, her face, her hair. She thrashed, clawing at the air, but the fire only grew.

With a final, unearthly shriek, Lady Red burst apart in a violent explosion of fire and ash. The blast rocked the castle, sending a hot wind rushing out the door. Then—nothing.

Silence.

All that remained was a single wisp of black smoke, twisting and curling before disappearing into the darkness.

The spirits, free at last, faded into the ether, their torment finally at an end. The castle exhaled a long, weary breath, its ancient stones settling. Lady Red was gone. And the curse was broken.

I stood, transfixed by what I had witnessed, my breath just out of reach as the walls steadied, returning to their familiar form. The stone floor was solid once more.

Joy ran to me, throwing her arms around me. "Claire!" she cried breathlessly. "Are you OK?"

Our tear-streaked cheeks mashed together as we embraced. I struggled to catch my breath, feeling the loss of Angus slice through me. My knees gave out as I cried unabashedly in Joy's arms, my body sagging against her lifelessly.

CHAPTER FORTY-SEVEN

Claire

I couldn't get out of bed the next morning. Every movement felt like wading through molasses. My body was heavy with sadness and my heart hollowed by pain. Angus's final words echoed in my mind, a haunting melody that refused to fade. I lay there, staring at the ceiling, unable to muster the will to face the day.

The hours blurred together. I missed my final class with Professor Stump—a petty concern compared to the storm raging inside me. Stump was going to give me a failing grade anyway, so what did it matter? I really couldn't make myself care about that considering the guilt and longing that gnawed at me relentlessly, leaving me paralyzed.

A soft knock at the bedroom door barely registered. When it opened, Effie stepped in, balancing a tray with a steaming bowl of soup and a hunk of fresh bread. "Lass, ye've nae eaten all day. This willnae do."

I managed to sit up, though the effort felt monumental. Effie set the tray on my lap and perched on the edge of the bed, her kind eyes full of concern. "I ken see yer hurting, but ye cannae let it consume ye."

I looked down at the soup, my throat tight. "I don't know how to move on, Effie. He's gone, and it feels like—like part of me went with him."

Effie reached out, placing a comforting hand on my shoulder. "Aye, grief's a heavy thing. But ye're still here, lass. That means there's still hope. Take it one step at a time. Start by eatin' this soup, and the rest will come together in time."

I nodded, a small flicker of gratitude breaking through the despair. I picked up the spoon, the warmth of soup a tiny balm against the cold ache in my chest. Effie stayed by my side, her presence a steady anchor in the sea of my sorrow.

Joy burst into the room shortly after Effie left, her excitement filling the space like a gust of wind. "Claire!" she exclaimed, barely pausing to catch her breath. "You won't believe what happened in class today!"

Startled by the urgency in Joy's voice, I sat up slowly, my energy drained but curiosity faintly piqued. "What happened?"

Joy leaned in, gripping my arm as if she needed something solid to keep herself from floating away in sheer shock. "It was Stump!" Joy said, her eyes wide. "He wasn't the same angry dictator we've been dealing with all summer. He—he shaved his mustache, Claire! And he spoke quietly, humbly even."

I raised an eyebrow. "Professor Stump?"

"Yes," Joy said dramatically, gripping her forehead. "Or should I say the ghost of Professor Stump because the man who taught our class today could not have been the same one we've suffered under all term."

My intrigue grew. "Go on."

Joy inhaled deeply, as if bracing herself. "Claire, he apologized. Like—openly. In front of the whole class. He came in looking like a man who'd just been visited by the spirits of Christmas past, present, and future, and then he actually apologized for being so, and I quote, 'unreasonably harsh' with us."

I nearly choked. "He what?"

"Oh, I'm not done!" Joy uncharacteristically wagged a finger. "Then he said he had reflected on his behavior and realized that, instead of nurturing our talent, he had been—wait for it—'stifling our creative spirits.' His words!"

My jaw dropped. "There is no way he said that."

"I swear on my sketchbook, Claire. Those words left his mouth! And that's not all. He—he smiled at us. Not the usual smug, self-satisfied smirk. An actual smile. Like a normal human person. I almost fainted."

I leaned forward, riveted. "What else did he do?"

"He encouraged us!" Joy pressed a hand to her heart like she was recounting a divine miracle. "He told us we should all continue pursuing art in the future."

"No."

"Yes." Joy's hands trembled in the air, as if she were trying to physically grasp the impossibility of it. "And then he helped me when my tools fell off the table. With patience and gentleness, Claire! It was like watching a hyena suddenly decide to befriend a herd of gazelles!"

I sat back, stunned. "Do you think the Ouija board is responsible?"

"Maybe," Joy whispered, as if afraid to jinx it. "Maybe the curse lifting. Maybe he had a near-death experience. Maybe he was possessed by a benevolent spirit. I don't know, but I am not questioning it."

I shook my head, still trying to process it. "I'm sorry I missed it."

Joy snorted, "It feels like a miracle."

I laughed a little, feeling my own heartache dissipate for a moment. "I guess it could happen."

Joy leaned back with a sigh of pure relief. "Honestly, Claire? After everything we've been through, I'll take it."

The two of us sat in stunned silence for a bit before Joy suddenly straightened. "Oh, and did I mention? He told us that everyone would be passing, and then—get this—he thanked us for a great semester and wished us a safe trip home!"

I blinked, trying to reconcile the image of the belligerent Professor Stump with his unexpected transformation. "He *thanked* you?"

"Yes!" Joy sat on the edge of my bed, her enthusiasm undeterred by my subdued demeanor. "It was like he was a completely different person."

I frowned, my thoughts clouded by unease.

Joy sat in contemplative silence for a moment before finally nodding. "At least we survived Stump's class." She forced a small, hopeful smile. "That's something, right?"

I nodded faintly, but the unease in my chest lingered, refusing to be soothed.

Compassion slid over her features. "I'm so sorry you're hurting, Claire. I wish there were something I could do."

I tried to smile as I patted her arm, grateful for her concern and care. "I appreciate you, Joy. I'm just glad we're going home."

She nodded. "Everything's going to be OK. You have to believe that."

I searched her eyes, hoping she was right.

CHAPTER FORTY-EIGHT

Claire

Our semester ended with an emotional farewell to the castle. Gone were the shadows that had lurked in its corners, the unnatural chill that had crept through its halls. No more eerie whispers in the dead of night, no restless spirits bound by Lady Red's wrath.

Sunlight poured through the arched windows, illuminating the stone walls with a golden glow. Outside, I noticed the garden bursting into color—roses and foxgloves stretched toward the sky, ivy curled lazily around the trellises, and heavy boughs of the orchard trees swayed gently in the morning breeze.

On my last morning, I stood at the edge of the garden, my bare feet pressing into the cool, dew-kissed grass. The air was warm, fresh with the scent of earth and blooming flowers. Birds trilled sweet melodies from their perches, filling the air with song. The wind, which had once howled with an unnatural fury, had softened into a playful whisper through the leaves.

I inhaled deeply, relishing the fresh morning air. It was as if the castle itself had released centuries of suffering and was finally at peace.

I met Effie in the small garden, where dew still clung to the flowers. "Ahh, just listen to that, lass." She was standing beneath a towering hawthorn tree, her hands on her hips, her face glowing with quiet joy.

She was dressed in a patchwork apron, her silver hair pinned up loosely. Effie looked more alive than I'd ever seen her.

"No more wailing, no more shadows creeping about," Effie continued, glancing around with deep satisfaction. "Just the sound of birds and the wind in the trees—proper castle sounds, if ye ask me." She smiled at me, eyes twinkling. "Told ye the place had a good heart under all that darkness."

I chuckled, stepping closer. "You were right, Effie. It feels alive now. Like it's waking up."

"Aye." Effie knelt beside a bed of violets and ran her fingers through the petals, her movements reverent. "The land knew it was cursed. It felt the weight of it. And now?" She took a deep breath, shaking her head in wonder. "Now it can breathe."

I crouched beside her, letting the damp grass soak into my fingertips. I had never noticed the deep richness of the soil, the way the morning light turned the flowers into tiny stained-glass windows.

"It's beautiful," I murmured.

"Aye, this place has taken a liking to ye, Claire. Ye helped set it free."

I swallowed the lump in my throat and smiled, thinking of the garden at home and eager to get back there.

Effie grinned and stood with a groan. "Och, my knees aren't what they used to be. Come on, lass. I'll not have ye standing here like some poetic heroine." She handed me a small, weathered pendant. "The curse is gone, lass," she said softly, her eyes glistening. "The spirits are at peace. Ye did that. Ye faced what others couldnae, and I'll always be proud of ye."

My eyes filled with tears as I hugged Effie tightly. "I couldn't have done it without you. I still really don't know exactly what I did, but thank you for believing in me."

"Yer light is powerful, lass. Never forget that."

We parted with promises to keep in touch. As I left the castle, I asked Angus, whatever remained of his spirit, his essence, to please give me a sign that he was OK, wherever he was now. My heart felt heavier and fuller than I'd ever known. I finished reading Diorval and I could relate to the ending. Like the book's main character, Emily, I was leaving behind a part of my heart to a soul who belonged to another place and time. And like her, I chose to carry on, knowing that my life was meant to be lived to the fullest, just as it was.

The flight home ended with goodbyes to my cohort and plans with Joy to hang out whenever we could. "You inspire me, Claire. I learned how to be strong from you."

"I feel the same way about you, Joy." I studied her for a moment, grateful that she had been with me on this journey.

As Joy and I parted after a hug, Vic approached us.

Vic gave me a hearty slap on the back. "Thanks for an unforgettable semester, kid. Never stop being you."

"Likewise," I nodded with an appreciative grin.

Barry rushed up to me in his customary way and threw his arm around my shoulders. "I'll be watching for your name in lights, Claire. You're crazy talented. Please never stop painting."

I replied, "Thank you. Good luck with everything, Barry."

He sent me off with a wink and a wave.

An hour and a half later, I was on the familiar streets of home, where Mom, Dad, Gini, and Grandma awaited me.

A barrage of hugs greeted me at the door, and it felt amazing to have been missed.

That night, my mom cooked a delicious dinner for us all, and the house was filled with conversation, laughter, and the comforting aroma of my favorite foods. "I'm so happy you're home safe," Mom said to me after dinner while nearly squeezing the life out of me in another bear hug. "We missed you, Claire. But I learned something while you were away, and that is that you've got this."

"Thanks, Mom. I learned that too, and I missed you guys so much. It's good to be home," I said, my eyes closed in total bliss as Mom squeezed me.

My dad cleared his throat loudly. "Share, please," he said, his eyes twinkling. They engulfed me in a group hug that Gini and Grandma soon joined, and it lasted until we were completely dissolved in a fit of giggles.

"What do you think of throwing a couple of your paintings into the mix next time I make my rounds?" Dad asked me as we enjoyed Mom's homemade cheesecake.

"You mean to sell them?" I asked, my eyes wide in surprise.

"They're that good," Gini chimed in.

"Truly." Grandma nodded.

I inhaled deeply, feeling completely flattered. "Yes, of course!"

Dad smiled. "I was hoping you'd say yes. Pick a couple that you don't mind parting with."

I felt myself blush a little. "Thanks, Dad."

Dad winked at me.

"If you ever need someone with a curbside sign to attract buyers to your art sales, let me know. I can dance," Grandma offered with a mischievous smile.

"Mother," Mom said, her fork midair as Grandma's never-ending antics made her pause pre-bite.

"We're good, Ivy," Dad agreed, shaking his head and trying to hide a smile.

"Grandma, you kill me," Gini said, laughing, barely able to contain the bite of cheesecake in her mouth.

"I am a really good dancer," Grandma insisted, rolling her shoulders in her signature move.

I laughed, holding my napkin over my mouth. "Stop, Grandma!"

During this moment of my family's silliness and warmth, I finally felt my inner turmoil leave. In its place, a sense of peace trickled in, peace like I had never known before. I realized I no longer needed to compare myself to anyone. The little voice in my head that had wondered if I was as good as Gini or good enough for my family, and the worry about whether my dream of being an artist was valid—it all evaporated. At last, I could accept that I was the unique person that I was meant to be. Not only was that good enough—it was pretty great.

CHAPTER FORTY-NINE

Claire

The first day of school arrived, back to high school—the start of my senior year. I returned with a quiet confidence that surprised even me. One crisp autumn afternoon, as I gathered my books outside after class, a voice called my name.

"Claire!"

I turned to see a dark-haired boy with piercing dark eyes holding something small and glittering in his hand. "Ye dropped this," he said, walking toward me and holding out my bracelet. "Looks like it's broken."

"Thank you," I murmured, taking it from him, my fingers brushing his. A strange feeling fluttered in my chest as our eyes met, something warm and familiar. "Oh, it is broken. It's been through a lot."

"I'm Evan," he said with a smile that set off his dimples. "Sorry about yer bracelet, but it's nice to meet ye besides."

"Nice to meet you too," I replied, matching his smile. "I recognize your accent. I studied abroad in Scotland over the summer."

"Aye, that's what I'm as well, an exchange student. Did ye meet any Highlanders while ye were there?" His eyes twinkled at me as if he somehow knew the answer.

I blushed and looked at him from under my lashes. "Yes, I did."

He smiled again, deepening his dimples, and my heart began to beat just a little faster. "Plan to be surprised," Mom had said.

My future was full of promise.

ABOUT THE AUTHOR

Jennifer Schulz-Johnston is a fiction writer and play therapist originally from Eau Claire, Wisconsin. She has a Bachelor of Social Work from UW–Eau Claire and an MS in Mental Health Counseling from UW–Stout. She was the executive director of the community-based mental health clinic, Marriage and Family Health Services from 2016 to 2022. Prior to that, she worked alongside her husband, Tom, (now deceased) in that clinic, since 1998. Writing has always been her hobby and passion. Her family and late husband have inspired her storytelling, ongoing. She currently resides in Minneapolis, Minnesota. *The Widow's Blood* is her third novel, which completes The Widow's Trilogy. *The Widow's Garden* (2016) was her first novel, followed by *The Widow's Secret* (2024).